Just Yesterday
A Journey of Strength and Change

FELIX SHABA (PhD)

Disclaimer

This work is a blend of facts and fiction: while certain events, settings, and historical details are based on actual occurrences, others are entirely the product of the author's imagination. Characters, unless explicitly stated otherwise, are fictitious, and any resemblance to actual persons, living or dead, is purely coincidental.The intent of this work is to entertain and inform people, not to present a definitive account of actual events. Readers are encouraged to approach narratives with this understanding.

Dedication

This book is dedicated to the loving memory of my late parents, Mrs. Elizabeth Ibidun Shaba and Mr. Martin B J Shaba. Your unwavering support and endless love continue to inspire me daily. Although you may have gone, your presence resonates on every page of this book

Chapter One: Ayetoro

As the sun rose and the first light of morning crept through the holes in their tiny home's mud walls, Shetan awoke from his slumber on the multifunctional tarpaulin he had stretched across the corridor. He had positioned himself between the centre of the passage and the perimeter, and he tightened his worn blanket over his body, feeling the chill of the harmattan penetrating the cloth. He moaned sleepily as he sat up, clearing his eyes to remove the sleepiness and observing the dim illumination of the awakening village.

It must already be six o'clock, he told himself. Although there was no clock in the house to prove the accuracy of the time, his body system had been so regulated that, no matter what time he slept, he could never miss waking up around that time. Mr Agbaje, his father, had gone to the farm before Shetan woke up from the multi-function tarpaulin on which he slept. His father bought the large spread sack to dry his farm produce, primarily cocoa and melon. While it was used to dry the produce during the daytime, it served as Shetan and his siblings' sleeping mat at night.

Mama Enitan was preparing for her day's work when Shetan woke up to prepare for school. Whenever she did not go to the farm to meet her husband, it was either because she had something to do at home or she wanted to work as a labourer to supplement the meagre output from their subsistence farming. She often joined other women who needed assistance planting or harvesting their farm produce or worked at Mama Olu's quarry site, where stones were gathered and broken into pieces with a hammer to build houses.

Shetan had virtually no chores to do in the house in the morning. It was almost a taboo in their home for a male child to pick up the broom to sweep, let alone wash plates or fetch water. These types of jobs were categorised as domestic functions exclusively meant for female children. With three fully grown-up girls in the house, it would be considered a lapse on their part if their father found Shetan and his two younger brothers performing domestic duties such as sweeping or fetching water from the stream for the house.

The only time Shetan did some of such work was when his older sisters- Bimpe, Fisayo, and Odun- would go early to the farm to bring home items they would sell in the market. However, this was very rare, as they usually went to the farm together to bring such items home a day before the market day. Besides, their father did not tolerate or condone such negligence on the part of his daughters and never failed to show his displeasure anytime such was brought to his notice.

Although his sisters sometimes asked him to fetch drinking water or wash plates, he would never do these things of his own free will. He was either being threatened or reminded of an offence he had committed long ago that his parents must not know about!

An incident led their father to impose a final embargo on Shetan, fetching water for the house.

One evening, Bimpe called Shetan to go and get some drinking water from the stream.

"But Aunty," he began respectfully (*as it was taboo in the house and even in the entire village to call someone older than you by name.),* "why can't you go yourself since you know our father said

I should not be fetching water for the house again?"

Bimpe's smooth face immediately squeezed into wrinkles as she turned away from the plates she was washing to face him.

"Are you blind?" She yelled. "Can't you see that I am busy preparing food so that our parents can have something to eat when they return from the farm? Moreover, you know that Fisayo and Odun also went to the farm with them. Who do you want me to leave the cooking for?"

Her chest heaved as she spoke, making her faded old blue wrapper sway uncontrollably on her body. At that instant, as though in agreement with her, the fire under the pot crackled loudly, followed by a hissing sound caused by the overflow of the boiling water into the fire. After contemplating the situation, Shetan grudgingly took the bucket from the back of the door that led to the dilapidated kitchen and headed to the stream.

"Make sure you return on time; as you can see, it's getting late already." Bimpe cautioned in a more relaxed tone that betrayed her anxiety.

He nodded without looking back. In his mind, he knew that she was not concerned about the time of day but wanted him to return before their father came back from the farm.

Despite the village hosting the local government headquarters and a water corporation that served the state capital, Akure, and other major towns in the surrounding area, the people of Ayetoro village never enjoyed pipe-borne water. They only had the big pipes laid through the village to the state capital. Except for the staff of the corporation who lived in the official quarters beside St John's Catholic Church, the entire village still had to go to the streams to fetch water.

If they were lucky and the staff in the quarters happened to forget to lock their detached bathroom building, the children would stealthily slip in to collect water. However, if caught, the staff would promptly chase them out, denying them access to the water source or pouring away the one they had already fetched.

On his way to the stream, Shetan passed through the only primary school in the village and saw some boys playing football on the field. He decided to watch for a few minutes. It was a game he loved so much, but he dared not touch a ball with his leg. Since the day his mother came to the field to beat and strip him naked in the presence of other players and spectators, Shetan vowed never to play football ever again! Before then, Mama Enitan had warned her son several times never to see playing football as a career.

"Has anyone ever emerged as a football star from this village or its surroundings?" she would always ask him.

But when she realised that merely denying him his dinner and her husband asking him to kneel on top of the small pebbles in front of the mud house could not stop his passion for the game, she resolved to take a more drastic step to deter him from using the slightest opportunity to run out of the house to the football field.

On that fateful evening, Shetan told his mother he was attending church for catechism class. At first, the woman was surprised and wondered why she had not heard her husband announce in the church the previous Sunday that there was going to be a catechism class for his age group! She told herself that maybe the announcement was made when she was busy controlling the children who were running up and down in the church.

Thirty minutes after he had left for church, Mama Enitan could still not believe that there was a catechism class that day. She knew when any of her children were lying to her. There were times when she gave them a long rope to pull, but whenever they took it for granted, she made them aware that although she had never known the four walls of a school in her lifetime, she had been able to develop some vital instincts through experience that the highest school on earth can never offer. So, she decided to trace him to the church to satisfy her curiosity. She wasn't surprised to see the doors of the church closed from afar, and she did not need a prophet to tell her that her second son was among dozens of children right in the field opposite the church, playing football!

Shetan's eyes were following one of the opponents coming closer to the goalpost when he felt someone grab his knickers from behind. Initially, he thought it was one of the boys watching the game trying to stop him from saving the ball from scoring, so he decided to brush off the hand with his left fist. He almost entered the ground when he looked back and saw his mother holding him! Caught between saving the shot fired by Gbenga and the impending doom that was about to befall him, Shetan tried to dive to catch the ball that was heading towards the left corner of the post, but his mother's grip would not allow him! The hand that gripped him pushed him out of the goalpost, and the ball went right through the bamboo goalpost! The opponents shouted for joy... "It is a goal!"

She gave him the beating of his life right on the field in the presence of everyone. As Shetan tried to escape the grip of his mother, his ragged knickers shredded into pieces! The entire crowd on the field burst out laughing, and for weeks, he was the talk of the village.

This time around, he promised to watch the game for just a few minutes before heading towards the stream. Rather than placing the bucket on the floor, he held on to it so that the temptation to join them and play wouldn't arise. He felt he could still spare a few minutes to watch the match before racing to the stream. After all, his parents should still be on the farm, and there is no one to monitor him.

The game was so interesting that Shetan forgot himself on the field. Before he realised where he was, the boys were already leaving one after the other, and the remaining few decided to end the game as it was getting dark. Though both sides promised to defeat each other, the match was still a goalless draw when darkness overshadowed the entire pitch. That was when Shetan remembered that he was holding an empty bucket in his hand! He looked around to see if he could find anyone to escort him to the stream, but no one was ready to go with him as they all dreaded Baba Jabo, an herbalist who lived just a few meters away from the stream.

With no one to escort him, he raced through the lonely path amidst the sound of myriad insects and other nocturnal creatures to the stream, his heart in his mouth. Without hesitation, he dipped the iron bucket into the stream and drew it out with his last ounce of courage. He did not even wait to check whether the water was clean before placing the bucket on his head and hurrying home.

His father, who was always the last person to return from the farm in the entire village, had already got home before Shetan. However, Mr Agbaje wouldn't have noticed his absence if not for the fact that he needed him to go and buy snuff for him. At first, his sisters pretended they did not hear when their father called Shetan from where he was sitting in his wool chair in front of the house. Though Bimpe told their mother, who had arrived some minutes before her husband, that she had sent him to get some drinking water, nobody dared tell the man where they had sent him! After he asked a second time, Mama Enitan summoned the courage to tell her husband that he had been sent to get some drinking water from the stream.

"Bimpe! Bimpe!" Mr Agbaje called in a row.

"Yes, Ita (as their father is called in their local language)." The poor girl answered timidly with her head lowered.

"Can you tell me the reason why you or Fisayo couldn't fetch water when you woke up this morning?" Mr Agbaje demanded.

"Um, um, um..." Bimpe stammered; she was still searching for an appropriate excuse when her father's angry voice slammed down on her.

"Keep your mouth shut! I have told you people time and again that you girls must make sure water is always in this house!" he roared.

" But Ita, we went to the stream yesterday morning to fetch water and were surprised that it had already finished," Bimpe argued, avoiding his eyes.

"Even if the entire village were to pay us a visit, I don't think they would be able to finish up the water so suddenly like that," Mr Agbaje retorted.

Fisayo was about to add her voice when Mr Agbaje asked them to get out of his sight. They were about to leave his presence when Shetan entered with the bucket of water. He was surprised that neither his father nor his mother asked him why he was late. He quietly consumed his dinner, and from then on, none of his sisters ever asked him to fetch water in the house for a very long time.

Bathing in the morning was not something that the primary and secondary students in Ayetoro and its neighbourhoods often liked to do, not even at that time of year when there was harmattan. It was the norm for almost all the children in the entire village to wake up in the morning, wash their arms up to the elbow and their legs up to their ankles, pour some water on their heads, wash their faces, and set off to school. Reports even showed that some teachers, mostly Miss Opelenge, did the same thing during severe harmattan weather! As usual, Shetan poured some water into a calabash bowl to perform the ablution at the back of their mud house.

The only cream Shetan grew up to meet in the house was *Adinagbon*, a locally made liquid extracted from palm kernel, which served as both body and hair cream for the entire family and, at the same time, acted as medication for stomach aches.

Shetan couldn't remember the last time he had a bath with soap. The only thing he enjoyed when coming back from Ikoshe, their cash crop farm, on Saturdays or during the holidays, was the herbal leaves he used to wash off all the dirt from his body in the stream. This was also the place where they fetched water for cooking and drinking on the farm. Whenever he felt like taking a soapy bath, he would gather the *irebu nawa* leaf, soak it in water, and squeeze it until it became foamy. He would then use it like a sponge to scrub his body from head to toe, rinsing off in the same stream that provided their drinking water.

Besides curing fever through bathing with its leaves, this particular plant was also used for purging. Occasionally, Mr. Agbaje would gather the leaves on the farm, squeeze them into a bowl until the water turned green, and then add a little salt. He would divide the mixture into small calabash bowls for himself and his sons to drink before starting the day's work. Shetan and his younger brothers despised this ritual because of the bitter taste. On such days, they knew they would eat late on the farm, as Mr. Agbaje wanted the herbs to take effect in their systems before they had their meals.

He picked up the *Adinagbon* cream and rubbed his face and body with it. He did not even bother to comb his hair, even if he wanted to; where would he get a comb from?

Mama Enitan's room served multiple purposes. The back of the door functioned as storage for farm produce, while the room also served as where Shetan kept his school uniform.

Shetan raised his mother's pillow and brought out his school uniform. This was the only uniform he had been using since he gained admission to secondary school. After five consecutive terms, the same white shirt and black knickers his father had bought for him since his first term in school were still what he wore to school!

It took his father five weeks after resumption to buy the uniform for him. Not that Mr Agbaje was unwilling to, but he could not raise the money to buy the two yards of white for the top and one and a half yards of black material for the shorts. The day his father handed the uniform to him, that Saturday evening in October, he was told point-blank not to expect any clothes for Christmas. That was how Shetan missed the once-a-year gift their father usually gave all the children each year!

Shetan quickly put on his uniform without minding how rough it was. The white shirt, once immaculate and neatly pressed, now displayed signs of its dedicated use. Remnants of food particles were visible on it, as well as persistent reminders of constant use. The collar, previously crisp and meticulously ironed, now sagged slightly, its structure weakened by the passage of time and repeated washing. The threads protruding from the seams at the hem serve as visible proof of the garment's long-lasting use. The uniform, worn and faded at the buttocks from countless hours of play and study, bore the quiet dignity of a well-loved companion on the journey through five rigorous academic terms.

There were times he even had to wear it at home if he washed his only play clothes. The only clothes he had besides the school uniform and the play clothes were the ones he wore to church every Sunday, and he dared not use them to play at home. How could he even get the church wear when his mother kept it for him in her metal box in his father's room? Where would he tell his mother he was going when it was not a Sunday? It was strictly for church, just as the uniform was for school purposes only.

Even though he patched his knickers at the back, he still had his shirt tucked in, as Mr Faginte, the school principal, never forgave any student caught flying their shirt. According to the principal, there were five offences he detested more than anything else. The most grievous of these was stealing. In his words, *"stealing is against all moral and religious teachings one can ever think of; thus, a thief is a thief irrespective of what he stole."* As a result, any student caught stealing—whether on school grounds or even at home, should the case be reported to him—faced immediate expulsion. Not only that but the names of such students were circulated across neighbouring schools to ensure that no one would admit a thief into their school.

As a consequence, students were always very careful not to covet what wasn't theirs, let alone take anything that didn't belong to them. The least among the sacrilegious offences, however, was improper dressing. This included flying collars and shirts, baggy knickers, short skirts, unkempt hair, painted nails, and failure to wear the recommended school sandals. Mr. Faginte was particularly strict about the issue of sandals. He preferred that his students come barefoot to school rather than wear sandals that did not meet his specifications. Only brown rubber or leather sandals were acceptable.

Any student caught violating these rules faced severe consequences. Not only would they be required to work on the school farm for three days, but they would also receive twelve strokes of the cane in front of all the other students during the morning assembly. This public punishment served as a reminder of the strict discipline upheld under Mr. Faginte's leadership, and the fear of it kept the students in line.

Shetan usually stopped at Mr Okoro's house on his way to school. Evans, Mr Okoro's first son, was his classmate and best childhood friend. They have been close friends since their primary school days. Their closeness was so tight that, to this day, many people still mix up their surnames. They understood each other so well that people wondered if they were not twins.

Shetan's parents were not initially comfortable with their son choosing an Igbo boy as a friend. As they always told him, *"Igbos can do anything to make money, and if care is not taken, your so-called friend will sell you to make money one day."* However, when Mama Enitan realised there was nothing, she could do to stop her son from being close to Evans, unlike the football case, she decided to leave him to his fate. One major thing that relieved Shetan's parents was attending the same Catholic Church as the Okoros. Still, they resolved to keep an eye on his activities with Evans.

Evans' parents were more financially stable than Shetan's. Apart from the cocoa farm they had, their main job was trading. The wife sold tobacco snuff, while the husband dealt with okirika (used clothes) and a few other daily necessities. They had a shop in front of their house but took their wares to the Owena and Alade markets every five days. The Alade market came a day after the Owena market.

Most mornings, whenever Shetan was fortunate enough to get to Mr Okoro's house in time, he ate his breakfast at his friend's house; even when he was a bit late, there were times when his bosom friend would purposely delay eating so that he could share his food with him. However, that morning was another unlucky day for Shetan, as Evans had just finished a bowl of *utarra akpu* and *olugbu* soup left from dinner the previous night when he arrived. Though he was unhappy that he missed another opportunity to have breakfast, he knew his stomach would remain empty till break time. He wondered if his friend had not rushed his food so that he would not have shared it with him.

Chapter Two: Stunted Dreams

They arrived at school some minutes before the bell rang for them to complete their daily tasks. The boys from classes one to three were assigned to cut the grass while their female counterparts swept the classrooms and the school surroundings. With a sense of purpose, the students dispersed, each group heading towards their assigned duties. The boys, eager to demonstrate their skills, picked up their blunt machetes and got to work. Their laughter mingled with the sound of metal hitting grass as they cut the overgrown grasses. Nearby, the girls swept stray leaves and dirt with their brooms, creating tidy trails behind them. Form four students, the highest level in the school at that time, were tasked with overseeing the morning duties.

At exactly 7:40 am, the school bell rang again, and like soldiers, the students were expected to leave whatever they were doing and run to the assembly ground right in front of the principal's office. Within a few minutes, they all lined up in their respective positions, each class according to its height in ascending order. Each class had two rows: one for the boys and the other for the girls. The teacher for each class was usually the last person behind the class, and they were expected to stand at the back of the last two students to maintain orderliness.

The principal considered it ineptitude on the part of any teacher who failed in this responsibility; he was so serious about this that there was a day he asked the form four teacher to go and kneel in his office because he could not maintain discipline while the principal was addressing the students! This caused a lot of eyebrow-raising in the school, but nobody dared challenge Mr Faginte for his actions.

It was an unusual sight to see the principal leading the morning assembly. Such occasions were rare, as he rarely ventured to the assembly ground in the early hours, let alone took charge of the proceedings. But whenever he appeared on the assembly ground in the morning, there must have been something serious he needed to sort out; it was either that he had an important message to pass on to the students, or he had caught one or two students who had flouted the rules and wanted to punish them in the presence of other students on the assembly ground.

The last time he conducted the assembly was the second week of this term when he suspended all the members of class four for a week. They were welcomed back to the school after the expiration of their suspension with twelve strokes of the cane and a day of hard labour on the school farm – which he supervised himself. Despite all the punishments they went through, none of the twenty-two students owned up or mentioned the name of the student who hissed when the biology teacher entered their classroom to teach them.

The assembly ground went dead as soon as they finished singing the National Anthem. They were all quiet and pondering in their minds what could be the reason why the stern-looking principal decided to conduct the assembly himself. They needed not to be told; his facial outlook said it all; some students would not find his presence there that morning palatable.

"Morning, students," he said.

"Good morning, sir," they all answered.

He paused for a few seconds, and it was as if heaven stood still for those moments, as one could easily hear the footsteps of ants walking around the field in search of food! Even the air around the assembly ground seemed to pause! Who dared to cough when the principal was addressing them? No one had ever attempted it.

He cleared his throat and continued. "As you all know, I have never conducted the assembly myself without a good reason. This morning…" He paused once again as if to create more suspense for the students. The way Shetan's heart was pounding, he knew that whatever the reason for the principal's presence that morning was, it had something to do with him! He hardly felt that way, and whenever such unusual fear came upon him, he knew trouble was looming but couldn't yet fathom the source. He was still pondering this in his mind when the principal cleared his throat once again. This brought his attention back to the assembly ground. He resolved within himself that he was ready to face whatever it was that brought the principal to the assembly ground that morning.

"This morning," the principal continued, "I am here to send back home those who think that we are still in the era of Obafemi Awolowo when education was free, and every Dick and Harry was allowed to go to school. As you all know, since the military took over almost a year ago, everything has changed. Education is now meant for those who can afford to pay the fees, and not every one of you is expected ever to see the four walls of schools."

At that point, Shetan knew his worst moment had come at last!

"Therefore," the principal continued. "Those who do not have the means should find other things to do, such as farming, tailoring, or becoming a motorbike mechanic. Education is not by force, and those who fail to understand this continually give me the trouble of coming to the assembly early in the morning. Imagine this is exactly seven weeks after the resumption, and with just four weeks to the examination, some students still feel that it is taboo for them to pay their school fees.

Shetan looked around and saw some students who were already gazing at him. He had been a regular defaulter; today, he would surely not disappoint them. It was as if the ground should open and swallow him up.

The principal brought out an exercise book in which he had listed the names of the debtors. He called out the names of the debtors in Class One. There were five in total - three boys and two girls. Four of them raised their hands and informed the principal that their parents had given them the money that morning, and they intended to pay it after the morning assembly. He asked them to walk immediately into the bursary office, make the payment, and return to the assembly with the receipt. The principal then turned to the only boy left in Class One.

"Can you tell me why you haven't paid your fees yet?" the principal demanded, his voice sharp with fury.

The boy shifted uncomfortably. "My mother said she would come and make the payment today."

The principal's gaze snapped towards the gate. A woman was walking through, but something about her movement struck him as strange. He paused, watching her closely, then turned back to the boy, his suspicion growing.

"Is that your mother entering through the gate?" he asked, his voice now colder and more intense.

In a joyful mood, the boy answered yes. He asked the boy to go and meet his mother and take her to the bursary to make the payment. The boy felt relieved and raced to meet his mother.

The principal then moved to the next class. As expected by all at the assembly, Shetan was the first person to be called, and it was no surprise to them that he was the only debtor in the whole of class two! When the principal checked through the list in his hands again and realised he was the only one, he asked him to step aside as his case was exceptional. The two students who were called in classes three and four were absent from school. He told their class members to inform them not to return to school until they had paid their fees. He promised to check their classes and assembly grounds from time to time to ensure they complied with his order.

"If any of those debtors are seen in the school without paying their fees, I will ensure I punish all class members who harbour such debtors," he roared.

Shetan looked like a condemned prisoner waiting for execution. Imagine being the only debtor on the ground among one hundred and thirty-six students! To cover up the tension, he began to scratch the ground with his big toe; he usually did this whenever he found himself in any embarrassing situation.

The principal watched the drama with bemusement; he wondered why a family in such a high poverty level could ever dream of sending their child to school to face such ridicule rather than asking him to follow them to the farm or learn a trade. But *"is it a must for a child in that poverty level to go to school when there are so many menial jobs such a child could pursue? Definitely no! I must put an end to this,"* he vowed to himself.

The whole assembly waited quietly to see what the principal would do. He cleared his throat once again, shook his head, and said, "The record shows that it has become a norm for you not to bother paying whatever levy the school comes up with until you are forced to do so."

He looked at Shetan from head to toe and wondered whether he had ever seen such a high level of poverty in his life!

"You have become a perpetual debtor to the school, and if we had three or four of your type, the school would have closed down by now! Since I have known you in this school, you have kept the number one position on the school's debtors list. Though you are also performing very well in your academics, gone are those days when education was meant for everyone. Our record also shows that no matter how small a levy is, you have never paid it willingly unless you are punished or sent home to meet your parents," he stated.

He suddenly halted mid-sentence, his voice dropping to a hushed tone as he asked Shetan to move closer. For Shetan, it felt as though invisible burdens weighed down his legs, and every step was a struggle against an unseen force. Yet, despite the heaviness, he found himself standing before the principal in a matter of seconds, as if propelled by some mysterious force.

Mr Faginte's stern gaze bore into Shetan, demanding his full attention and compliance. A knot tightened in Shetan's stomach, the weight of the principal's presence pressing down on him. He braced himself, knowing something was about to happen—something he wasn't sure he was ready for.

The principal's words cut through the tense silence, each one sharp and deliberate, heavy with authority and expectation. "Well?" he demanded, his tone brokering no argument.

"Turn around, Shetan," the principal commanded, his voice cutting through the silence like a knife. "Remove your hands from your buttocks."

Shetan's heart raced as he obeyed, his hands trembling slightly as they fumbled with the fabric of his shorts. The two blue mischievous eyes embroidered on the black fabric seemed to mock him, their playful smirk at odds with the gravity of the situation.

Once Shetan had complied, the principal ordered him to face the assembly, exposing the offending garment to the scrutiny of his peers. Though familiar to many, the sight of Shetan's patched shorts ignited a wave of laughter that rippled through the crowd, breaking the tension that hung heavily in the air.

Sensing the assembly's descent into chaos, the principal swiftly intervened, calling the timekeeper to ring the bell incessantly until order was restored. As the metallic chime echoed across the school grounds, a collective sigh of relief swept through the assembly, providing a reprieve from the weight of the moment.

Within moments, the raucous laughter dissolved into an uneasy silence, and the assembly ground returned to its solemn state. The principal's piercing gaze bore into Shetan, his eyes like twin flames burning with intensity as he asked his question.

"Who is your father?" The principal's voice cut through the stillness, each word dripping with authority and expectation.

Shetan hesitated, his heart pounding in his chest as he turned to face the principal, his hands instinctively moving to shield the patched fabric of his shorts from view. But before he could utter a word, the principal's booming voice shattered the silence once more.

"Do you want to tell me that you are deaf?" the principal's words reverberated through the air, his tone a mixture of disbelief and frustration.

Shetan's throat tightened, his mind racing as he searched for the right words to respond. A hot flush of embarrassment washed over him, and his cheeks burning with shame under the weight of the principal's scrutiny. But beneath the fear and humiliation, a spark of defiance flickered to life within him, a stubborn determination to stand his ground in the face of adversity.

I repeat, "Who is your father?"

Summoning every ounce of courage he possessed, Shetan squared his shoulders and met the principal's gaze head-on. Though his voice quivered with uncertainty, his resolve remained unwavering as he spoke.

"Mr Agbaje," he answered pitifully.

The principal's words resonated throughout the assembly grounds; each syllable was weighted with a stern determination that tolerated no dispute. His gaze raced over the sea of faces before him, his eyes gleaming with a furious desire to uphold his principles.

"I have told you, students, time and time again," the principal's voice rang out, commanding attention and respect in equal measure, "I hate seeing paupers in my school. No matter how brilliant a student might be, they must still meet some basic requirements before I recognise them as my student."

His declaration hung heavy in the air, casting a shadow over the assembled students as they absorbed the weight of his words. For Shetan and others like him, it was a harsh reminder of the barriers between them and their dreams, a stark reality threatening to dim the flame of hope burning within their hearts.

But even in the face of such adversity, Shetan refused to be cowed. Though the principal's words stung like a slap in the face, he remained steadfast in his resolve, determined not to see himself as a victim.

To emphasise the kind of student he envisioned for his school, the principal called out Shonu, whose magnificent appearance as he strode to the front of the assembly was impossible to ignore. With a haughty glance in Shetan's direction, Shonu's presence spoke volumes about the standard of excellence the principal sought to uphold.

"Look at this student, and I want you to compare what you are wearing with his," he said.

Without being told, even a blind man would have known that Shetan was wearing mere rags! The principal looked at him once again and shook his head. Other teachers could not help but sympathise with the humiliation the no-nonsense principal was inflicting on him.

I wonder how you managed to pass through primary school up to this level with your state of poverty. "You should thank Obafemi Awolowo, who implemented free education in the West before the military took over and introduced fees at all levels," he continued. "I want to assure you that today will undoubtedly mark the end of your days within these school walls. However, before I bid you farewell to this educational environment, I have a special gift in store for you. This token will serve as a lasting memory of your final day here," he announced in a solemn tone.

The principal called out the teacher in charge of discipline.

Dr Do-good, as he was fondly called, was the dreaded enforcer of discipline. He was known for his ruthless hand and unforgiving gaze. His presence alone sent shivers down students' spines, and his reputation preceded him like a dark cloud of dread. He was a wizard when it came to dealing with offenders. He was so skilled in the act of smacking and punishing students that principals in other schools hired him for a fee to discipline their errant students! No one ever crossed his path as all feared him. Apart from the general belief that he studied how to smack students to a degree level (although nobody could authenticate the existence of such a course anywhere in the world), the students also believed that he was using some traditional powers to smack students because even if he did not raise his hand so high to hit a student, such a student would still cry. No student had ever escaped this except Bimbo, the daughter of Baba Jabo, one of the herbalists in the village.

Bimbo, Shetan's classmate, arrived late to school one morning, accompanied by several other tardy students. As they approached the school gate and saw Dr. Do-good stationed there, a sense of apprehension washed over them. Panicked, the other students turned on their heels and fled home, hoping to escape the consequences of their lateness.

However, Bimbo remained unfazed by the presence of the teacher on duty. With an air of confidence, she strode towards the gate, her head held high and her posture regal. Despite the urgent calls from her concerned friends warning her of Dr Do-good's watchful gaze, Bimbo paid them no heed. Instead, she continued her majestic advance, refusing to acknowledge any wrongdoing as she made her way onto the school grounds.

Dr Do-good's fury peaked when he witnessed Bimbo's nonchalant entry, devoid of remorse or respect. His anger flared further when she failed to greet him as she passed through the gate. "Come here!" he roared; his voice laced with anger. "How dare you stroll in here as if you own the place, knowing full well that you're late!"

His frustration boiling over, Dr Do-good demanded an answer from Bimbo, his patience wearing thin at her unyielding demeanour. "Yet, despite his escalating rage, Bimbo remained unfazed, her hands resting firmly on her hips as she continued to chew her gum with an air of defiance." This only served to stoke the flames of his anger, his irritation mounting with each passing moment.

Finally, unable to contain his annoyance any longer, Dr. Do-good made a decisive move. With a wave of his hand, he released the other latecomers, their punishment forgiven in light of Bimbo's blatant disregard for authority.

"I'll show you today how to make your way to school properly when you're running late," he declared.

"Now, I want you to run from here to the front of the assembly ground and kneel there until I arrive to dismiss the assembly."

Despite his fierce command, Bimbo remained unshaken by his threat as she walked towards the assembly ground with the same sense of triumph with which she had entered through the school gate.

When Dr. Do-good realised that Bimbo was not sober, he decided to take matters into his own hands. With a stern grip, he dragged her toward the assembly ground, where the students were waiting for him to make the announcement and disperse them since he was also the teacher on duty.

When other students saw how he forced Bimbo to kneel on the assembly ground, they knew she was in great trouble. Some of her friends were already crying for her! But what baffled most of them was that Bimbo remained unruffled.

"Silence!" He screamed. Suddenly, the assembly went dead.

"Good morning, students," he said.

"Good morning, sir," The students responded.

"Before I make the announcement for the day," he continued, "I am sure some of you, if not all, have been watching with interest and bewilderment the drama from the school gate to this assembly point. I need not remind you of the school's five commandments: lateness, being rude to your seniors, not to talk of your teachers, are some of them."

He reminded them of the penalty an offender faced for not feeling remorse. To him, such an attitude carried more weight than the offence itself, and he would never hesitate to deal with any student who broke any of the five rules and regulations. "As you all know," he continued, "nobody ever dares Dr Do-good. But this morning, I am going to show this little brat here that I remain who I am in this school and the whole of this environment," he stressed.

Bimbo remained utterly indifferent to Dr Do-good's words; her attention seemingly fixed elsewhere as she continued to chew her gum. Enraged by her disregard, the teacher dispatched a student to retrieve his special cane from the staff room. This particular cane, reserved for exceptional circumstances, was seldom brought out except in moments of utmost importance. The last time it had been wielded was two months ago when a class one student had caught a class four student smoking cigarettes in the school's pit toilet.

Ajayi had ventured to answer the call of nature when he noticed wisps of smoke billowing from the male lavatory. He rushed to call the health teacher, who caught Bolu with a packet of Benson & Hedges in his pocket and three butts he had just finished. The woman collected the cigarette butts and the box of Benson & Hedges as evidence and took the boy to the principal's office. Luckily for Bolu, the principal had gone for a three-day *All Principals' Conference*, which started that Wednesday. The vice-principal swiftly convened an assembly, summoning all the students to witness the consequences of Bolu's actions.

In a stern display of disciplinary action, the boy received twelve strokes of the cane and was tasked with uprooting two palm trees on the school farm as further punishment. It took him five grueling days to complete the arduous task, enduring the physical exertion and the weight of his transgression. Despite the passage of time, Bolu remained mystified as to how the vigilant female health teacher had uncovered his clandestine smoking activities in the male lavatory.

The boy rushed back with the cane. Not that there was anything special about it apart from the fact that the atori had some branches that made it penetrate any part of the body it touched; despite the simplicity of the cane, the students still believed that it was soaked with some concoctions, which made it so painful. Dr Do-good collected it from the student and asked Bimbo to stretch out her hand. Still undeterred, she extended her hand to receive the strokes. The students did not actually know how many she would receive, as Dr Do-good did not say either. But the surprising thing was that he suddenly stopped when all the students counted up to thirteen.

To the students' amazement, she showed no sign of discomfort, let alone pain! She was instead smiling! Unbelievable! So, Bimbo did not shed tears! Dr Do-good became angrier. He asked her to stretch out the other hand. As she stretched her hand, he examined the cane again to ensure it was the same ceremonial cane that all the students dreaded. He used his fingers to straighten the branches and told himself that she must shed tears this time around. As the cane descended upon Bimbo's left hand, the students counted aloud, their voices echoing through the assembly grounds. Eleven, twelve, the strokes rained relentlessly, but Bimbo remained resolute, her composure unbroken.

Dr. Do-good, sweating profusely, realised the futility of his efforts to elicit tears from the defiant student. With a heavy heart, he halted the punishment, the assembly erupting into a chorus of chants, "Bimbo! Bimbo!! Bimbo"!!! Speculations flew among the students, with some suggesting that her father had *cooked* her with a potent concoction to withstand pain. Others attributed it to the local ring she wore on her index finger when Dr Do-good was about to administer the punishment.

Uncertain of his next course of action, Dr. Do-good instructed Bimbo to proceed to his office and kneel in contemplation. The students hailed her as she walked royally towards the staff room. "She had destroyed the charm on the cane," one student shouted. But who dared break any of the rules that would warrant bringing out the *ceremonial* cane to test the student's claim?

Bimbo became the topic of each class and the news of the town. Some students came from neighbouring schools to see the strange lady who defied the 'consequential torture' law.

It was that same cane Dr Do-good went for that faithful morning when the principal told him to give Shetan what he called a *valedictory punishment*. The students, who had been apprehensive since the last time the cane was used, expected him to brave up like Bimbo, a 'girl for that matter'! Some students were happy that the ceremonial cane had come out once again. They had been curious since the day the cane did not work its usual wonders on Bimbo and had been waiting for the time their curiosity would be laid to rest.

Even Shetan had been waiting for that same day without knowing that the experiment would be on him. He tried to summon courage, knowing full well that all the students had been looking forward to this day. He thought that if a girl could receive almost twenty-four strokes of the cane and still be smiling, why couldn't he do the same? The principal asked him to lie down and instructed Dr Do-good to give him twelve strokes on his back and buttocks. The principal's commanding voice echoed through the assembly ground.

"Make sure you leave indelible marks on his back, a punishment that will serve as a lasting memory of his school days, so that anytime he looks at his back in a mirror—if he ever has the money to buy one in his lifetime," the principal commanded!

Shetan watched as justice was done to his back and buttocks. Despite his best efforts to steel his nerves, Shetan's resolve crumbled under the first strike of the cane, his cries echoing through the silent assembly ground. The pain, sharp and searing, overwhelmed him, leaving him gasping for breath and tears streaming down his cheeks. It was as if Dr. Do-good had poured his entire energy into those first few strokes, leaving Shetan broken and defeated in their wake.

As Shetan lay there, his back bearing the painful welts of the cane, the assembled students watched on with a myriad of reactions. Some were moved by the sight of his tears, empathising with his pain, and silently offering words of support. Others, however, found amusement in his distress, their whispers tinged with curiosity as to why a boy of his age would sob so openly.

With each lash of the cane, Shetan found himself lost in a whirlwind of thoughts, pondering the injustices he faced and the harsh realities of his circumstances. Tears streamed down his cheeks unabated, his mind consumed by the unfairness of it all. He did not even know when Dr Do-good stopped as the pain went on and on. Evans later told him the teacher added one extra when Shetan refused to get up.

But for Shetan, the tears flowed not just from the sting of the cane but from a more bottomless well of hurt and frustration. Even if the teacher had refrained from administering any punishment, would he not still cry? Could anyone endure the relentless humiliations he suffered at the hands of the heartless principal without shedding tears? It was a burden he bore alone—the weight of being the sole debtor in his class, the critical debtor on the school's list, and the poorest among his peers.

Once the principal was satisfied with the punishment that had been administered, he instructed Shetan to rise. "Take a good look around you at this school environment," he commanded sternly. "Promise me you won't set foot here again until you've settled your fees and shown a commitment to paying on time in the future."

Without waiting for a response, the principal continued, "Now, return to your class, gather your belongings, and leave the school premises immediately." With a heavy heart and aching back, Shetan staggered away from the assembly ground; his steps weighed down by self-pity. Each movement sent waves of pain rippling through his body as if hot pepper had been spread across his back. Slowly, he made his way to his classroom, his mind filled with a mixture of shame, resentment, and determination.

Meanwhile, the principal made further announcements, urging the students to return to their classes and resume their studies for the day. As the students dispersed, the echoes of Shetan's punishment lingered in the air, a sad reminder of the harsh realities of life within the school's walls.

As Shetan gathered his two eighty-page notebooks, meticulously divided into sections for his eight subjects, he couldn't help but taste the bitterness of his tears as they mingled with the memories of dashed dreams. Gazing at the drawings of two happy figures decorated in graduation gowns and caps adorning the front covers, he felt a pang of longing for the future he had once envisioned—a future now seemingly out of reach.

The tears flowed unabated down his cheeks, staining the pages of his notebooks as he contemplated the uncertain path ahead. The familiar four walls of the classroom, once a sanctuary of learning and hope, now loomed before him as a symbol of his shattered aspirations.

As Shetan stood at the threshold of the classroom, preparing to leave, he felt the weight of his decision heavy upon him. The temptation to take his chair and locker, symbols of his time within these walls, was strong, but the reminder that these belonged to the government and any attempt to claim them would be seen as theft served as a sobering deterrent.

As other students began to trickle into the classroom, their gazes filled with a mix of scorn and pity, Shetan couldn't help but feel a pang of isolation. Among them was one student in particular, whose satisfaction at Shetan's departure was thinly veiled. Though Shetan had never directly offended him, his mere presence posed a threat academically. The rivalry between Shetan and Shonu was fierce; their competition in subjects like English and Mathematics left no room for friendship. Being a city boy, he often saw himself as better than the boys in Ayetoro and harboured ambitions of academic superiority. Shetan's consistent performance had continually thwarted these aspirations.

If Shetan came first in English, Shonu would take first in Mathematics. No one in the class ever came first in both subjects. However, his leaving the school would now give Shonu the chance to dominate in both subjects, something he had craved so much. Shonu, who joined them from Akure when his father was transferred to the Water Corporation in the village, wanted to be seen as the most brilliant boy in the class. Despite his consistent performance, Shetan's presence had always cast a shadow over Shonu's ambitions, repeatedly thwarting his dreams of academic supremacy. Now, with Shetan's departure, Shonu saw an opportunity to finally claim the recognition he believed he deserved, free from the constraints of their bitter rivalry.

As Shetan stood in front of the classroom, grappling with the weight of his departure, Evans approached him with words of comfort and reassurance. Promising to check on him later that day, Evans offered Shetan a glimmer of solace amid his turmoil. Shetan would surely miss the company of his friend, who had been so kind to him. Evans was still consoling him when Mr Adebayo, their class teacher, entered the classroom to mark the register as the teachers do every morning. He was about to turn and go home when Mr Adebayo called him to the front corner of the class for a private chat with him.

"Why do you always find it difficult to pay your fees despite your excellent performance in class?" Shetan managed to hold back his tears for the first time, looking up at him with eyes red and swollen. "Sir, it...it is not intentional." He choked and swallowed hard. "My parents always try their best, only that I'm just being unlucky."

"Pele," Mr. Adebayo said, his tone laced with empathy. "Do everything you can to settle your fees and return to school. Education is the key to unlocking your potential and overcoming your current predicament. It's the pathway to success in life." With those words in mind, Shetan folded his books and headed home.

Ayetoro Police Station was directly opposite Owena United High School, just beside Idanre local government headquarters, and it was one of the largest police stations in the local government. Many thoughts came to his mind as he walked towards the gate. Amidst the bustling atmosphere of the early police parade, his attention was drawn to a particular officer jogging fervently with raised hands, clutching his gun and drenched in sweat.

Despite his predicament, the scene stirred a sense of empathy within him. Like him, he could sense that the officer was facing repercussions, perhaps for an action or inaction. Despite any differences in age or rank, he couldn't help but feel a twinge of pity for the officer. At that moment, a faint smile played on his lips as he acknowledged the universal truth that consequences spare no one, regardless of status or experience.

As he walked down the road to their mud house, the few people who met him on the way asked why he was heading home at that time of day, and they felt sorry for him when he told them he was sent home because of school fees.

Chapter Three: Faded Hope

The cracking sound of the kernels that went PA-PA-PA under Mama Enitan's hand-held stone mingled with the turmoil in her heart. As she skilfully picked out the nuts, her thoughts drifted to the stone itself—standing firm and resolute amidst the growing pile of broken shells around it. This was akin to the system that shaped her current state and that of others, stripping away their essence and leaving them broken and helpless.

"A woman's place is in the kitchen the moment she gets married… No matter what…" These words re-echoed in her head. She straightened up, looked around, and then back at her tattered clothes. Everything was bleak, a clear testament to poverty and this belief system.

"No, no, no," she muttered. "So long as my spirit remains strong within me, I can't be a waste." She shook her head vigorously, resisting the encroaching waves of depression. Her mind raced through the privations she endured and the disappointment she faced that morning on her way to Mama Olu's quarry. It was a menial job, but it offered some hope at the end of each day. The site owner had sent someone to tell her that she couldn't go due to a slight headache. As a last resort, she busied herself here rather than idling away the day, sulking. Sad memories of the past assaulted her, causing her to hiss intermittently as she fought back the tears.

"My children will never go through this, particularly these boys, as long as I live. Never will they suffer my fate and that of their father."

Just then, a ray of sunlight piercing through a hole in the iron roof seemed to dance on the back of her palm, as if placing a seal on her desire.

The gentle morning breeze rustled through the roof of the dilapidated kitchen, and her multicoloured head tie fluttered loosely behind her. She was thus preoccupied when the sound of Shetan's shuffling feet interrupted her cogitation.

"Iyan, how come you're still home by this time?" He asked in surprise.

He was about to follow up with more questions when he noticed his mother's hand suspended mid-air, still gripping the stone she had been using to crack palm kernels.

"Son," she choked as tears flowed freely from her sunken eyes, "I, I, I, knew this day would come. At this point, Shetan could no longer hold back the tears he had managed to conceal on his way home. It turned into a crying spree as they recounted their ordeals.

The first son was fortunate, benefiting from free education all the way through secondary school. But the day the announcement came that education would no longer be free was a sorrowful one for Mama Enitan.

Shetan had just completed his first-term year-one exams and eagerly awaited the end of the Christmas break when the country was abruptly thrust into turmoil on New Year's Eve due to the sudden military takeover. While many initially welcomed the move, hoping for an end to the rampant rigging and corruption that plagued the previous regime, the joy quickly turned to dismay for Mama Enitan and countless others. Learning that one of Buhari and Idiagbon's first actions was to abolish free education dealt a devastating blow to families. Despite promises to foster a disciplined society, the introduction of school fees imposed an additional burden on already struggling households, exacerbating the hardships brought on by the political upheaval.

The amount was not substantial, but for the Agbajes, gathering fifty Naira for the fees felt as challenging as asking a leper to display his ten fingers. In the impoverished community, every penny was a precious commodity, and scraping together even a small sum for education expenses was daunting.

"But how could life be so cruel and unjust to us? What kind of life is this?" These were the questions that echoed relentlessly in Shetan's mind as tears streamed down his cheeks. "Who should bear the blame for our poverty? Are my parents lazy or are they destined to remain poor in life?" Each question weighed heavily on his heart, stirring up a tumult of emotions as he grappled with the harsh realities of his circumstances.

Shetan could see Mrs Chinedu, their neighbour to the right, looking at them in the dilapidated kitchen and laughing. He desired to confront the woman but refrained from doing so to avoid causing more trouble and unnecessary attention from the villagers.

He hated the woman with passion since the day she called his mother a ragged woman. Even though he refrained from taking any physical action since she had two grown-up sons older than him, Shetan spent more than two weeks following her goats and chickens in the bushes. He was relieved one Friday afternoon when he came home from school and was on his way to set his mouse traps when he suddenly saw the bush shaking. At first, he thought it was a bush animal, but when he looked further, he realised it was Mrs Chinedu's goat. He looked for one of the best stones in his catapult bag and aimed at the left hind leg of the goat. Until now, Mrs Chinedu had not found out why her goat limped home!

After weeping for about two minutes, his mother put the small stone down and stood up to comfort her son. She used the tip of the wrapper she was tying on her chest to wipe her tears and those of her son. She gazed at her son as he left the kitchen and entered the mud house. She wondered if the white and black uniform would ever serve its primary purpose again.

Her love for Western education was so profound that it bordered on obsession with seeing her children achieve it, that people would always ask her, "Why didn't you go to school, seeing you love education this much?"

"My teacher's mother died the very day I was supposed to start school!" she would jokingly remark, humbly. "So, let my children do it on my behalf."

Shetan needed no prompting to know what to do next. He had just put on his farm clothes when his mother called him. He returned to meet her in the kitchen, and she was pleased when she saw him already dressed in his farm attire.

"I was just about to ask you to go and meet your father on the farm," she said, her tone gentle yet firm. "Now that you're ready, make sure you head there promptly. You can explain everything to your father; besides, you'll have the chance to eat there, as we don't have any food at home for you," she concluded, her voice calming and reassuring.

Mama Enitan was still crying when Shetan picked up his catapult and the small sack he used for pebbles and headed towards Ikoshe, their cash crop farm. It had always been his dream to significantly impact the lives of his parents, especially his mother. As he walked to the farm, myriad thoughts filtered through his mind. Although he knew what his father's response would be, he still could not imagine why fifty Naira could separate him from his dreams.

He knew how much his father detested embarrassment of any sort in his life and would do anything within his ability to avoid it. Somehow, it gave him a sense of hope as he recalled how his father managed a situation, he believed was worse than his present predicament.

There was this cantankerous woman dreaded by the villagers, whom they suspected of donating her husband to her witch coven because of the circumstances surrounding his death. The man was coming from Akure to Ayetoro and was about to exit the Akure-Ondo motorway into Ayetoro when a trailer from nowhere crushed him to death. The accident was so ghastly that the man was torn to pieces, and a shovel was used to scoop up his remains. This incident caused quite a stir in the entire village as Bamidele, who was a hunter, was considered a very loving man.

That afternoon, Mrs Arike Bamidele came up with her arrogant and malicious behaviour as she stormed into Mr Agbaje's humble mud house with her son. Her eyes were blazed with fury, and her clenched fists trembled in anger.

Upon reaching the doorstep, she didn't bother with the polite tap or the customary call of greeting. Instead, she pounded on the door with a force that echoed through the quiet streets. The wooden frame rattled under her assault as if protesting her intrusion. Ignoring any sense of decorum, she thrust the door open with a resounding crash, the hinges protesting the sudden violence. As she entered the passage, her voice rang out with a shrill intensity that shattered the tranquillity of the house. "Agbaje!" she bellowed, her words reverberating off the walls. "Where are you? Show yourself, you coward!"

Kunle was Fisayo's classmate in primary school. The source of this chaotic incident stemmed from a heated argument at the village school, where Fisayo had given a severe beating to the woman's son. It was rather unusual and embarrassing for a boy to be beaten by a girl, especially in such a public setting, and the humiliation of the defeat only served to stoke the flames of Mrs Arike Bamidele's anger further.

"I can't comprehend how a girl could beat up a boy to the extent of tearing his uniform into pieces and inflicting injuries all over his body!" the woman yelled. Loosening her wrapper a little, she tied it more firmly around her waist and tightened the knots.

Within minutes, some villagers gathered and began pleading with her to let go.

"Ejoo! Ejoo! Ejoo! The man is not home yet!"

When the woman heard these words, she went berserk instead of softening. She fetched a handful of sand with her fingers, poured some on her tongue, threw the remaining sand into the sky and screamed, "I swear by my ancestors that out of two things, one must happen today, except my Baba isn't my father, or I wasn't properly born! Unless he pays for his treatment and gets him a new uniform at once, this land will not accommodate two of us." Her face was a bizarre mask with bloodshot eyes flashing at everyone, forcing them to step back.

"Why would this girl even exchange words with the boy in the first place, let alone fight with him?" The onlookers murmured in low tones for fear of being overheard.

It was at this time that Mr Agbaje dragged his tired body home, only to be welcomed with a barrage of abuse from the woman that left him in confusion. For a moment, he ignored her, entered his room, and found out from his first wife what warranted such disgusting behaviour. He fell into deep thought, trying to figure out a solution when the woman's shrill voice cut him short.

"Agbaje, come out here, you coward! Don't think you can hide in there!" By now, a large crowd of villagers had gathered, curious and unsettled by her boldness. They were shocked by her rudeness, particularly her decision to address him by his first name instead of respectfully referring to him through one of his children's names.

Mama Enitan wanted to go and start a fight with her in annoyance, but was held back by her husband, who offered to go and meet the troubled woman.

He braced himself up and went out again to meet the woman who immediately pounced on him, grabbing his shirt tightly around the neck.

"Look, Agbaje, I'll not leave you until this matter is settled!" She boasted as the uncontrollable shower of spittle that left her mouth whenever she spoke rested on Mr Agbaje's chest.

"So, what do you want me to do?" he asked with a gentle tone, contrary to his impulse to beat her to a pulp, knowing that this would compound the situation.

"You must pay the twenty Naira I used to sew my son's uniform and another ten Naira for his medical treatment," the woman yelled.

Mr Agbaje's eyes widened in disbelief. "Twenty whole Naira just for a pair of khaki shorts and a shirt?" He spent eighty-five Naira to clothe his entire family last Christmas. He had the urge to argue with the woman but quickly dismissed the idea. "Give me three days to sell some produce and get you the money," he persuaded, not minding the woman's bad breath and strong body odour that violently assaulted his nostrils. But the woman was adamant.

Not knowing what to do, he asked Mama Enitan to bring out his two remaining goats as a last resort. All the children watched the drama, not knowing what their father wanted to do with the domestic animals. Even Fisayo, who was the cause of the entire situation, hid in the kitchen, crying profusely. The goats and the chickens were their supplementary sources of income, second only to the farm produce. Mr Agbaje rarely sold them; whenever he did, it was either for an emergency or a critical situation.

The only time Shetan could ever remember two goats being sold was when Odun, Shetan's immediate elder sister, was sick four years earlier. Her illness defied all the herbs in the village, and even the revered Baba Salami could not fathom the root cause of the ailment. It became apparent she would die if drastic steps were not taken. Left with no options, he sold two of his goats and raised the money for the hospital bills—where she was admitted for three days and treated for typhoid fever.

Mama Enitan went to the kitchen, tied the goats securely, and brought them into the passage.

"Now," said Mr Agbaje, turning to the woman. "Choose any of these that cover the cost of your bills."

The woman's breathing quickened in greedy excitement when she saw the goats. Letting go of Mr Agbaje's shirt, she licked her dry, rough lips repeatedly and tore the ropes tethering the two goats from Mama Enitan's hand.

"Agbaje, I'll bring you the change if there's any after I sell them," she growled, then hissed at everyone around. Tugging the goats behind her, she strutted back to her house.

Mama Enitan was furious and wanted to confront her, but her husband urged her to let the devil take her trouble away. To this day, she neither returned a kobo nor any of the goats. Some even claimed she kept the goats as her pets.

Fisayo braced herself for the inevitable consequence of her actions, expecting her father to summon her for a severe reprimand. However, to her surprise, Mr. Agbaje neither called her nor administered any punishment for what she had done. It was a departure from his usual disciplinary approach. Though aware her parents might bear repercussions for her actions, Fisayo felt no regret about confronting Kunle. His insults, mocking her as the daughter of poor parents, ignited a fierce determination within her. In her eyes, standing up for her family's honour outweighed any potential consequences, and She remained steadfast in her defiance, her determination unwavering. So, Shetan hoped this would be one of those moments.

The cash crop farm, named Ikoshe, lay approximately two miles from the village. Nestled amidst hilly terrain, its name derived from its elevated location, offering panoramic views that stretched as far as Akure and Idanre. Standing on the farm, one could behold the vast expanse of land—a testament to the beauty and grandeur of the surrounding landscape. The other two farms were cocoa plantations, and the only time Mr Agbaje went there was when he wanted to spray disinfectant on the cocoa seeds or during the harvest. They were mostly done at weekends when all his children, mainly the boys, would not be in school so that they could assist in fetching water and cooking on the farm. Besides those two periods, the food crop farm was where he went almost every day, except on Sundays.

Mr Agbaje was hardly at home during the week, except for the times he went to represent either the Catholic Church or his cooperative society at away meetings. There were also times he still went to the farm whenever he returned early from any of those meetings.

"Why not stay at home and rest?" Mama Enitan would ask him sometimes.

"I need to check the traps as they don't announce when they will have something for me." He would always answer her. Yet, the output from the farm was never enough to cater for the family.

The path to the farm was deserted, as Shetan expected. It was difficult to spot anyone heading to or returning from the farm at that hour, as most farmers would still be diligently working before the sun's intensity became unbearable. The dry harmattan season further contributed to the quietness, making some people choose to stay at home. Even the usually active squirrels and birds were absent during that time, having already foraged for food early in the morning and sought refuge from the scorching sun.

Shetan walked the solitary path to the farm, his mind preoccupied with various thoughts. One recurring idea that lingered was Mr Adebayo's advice to pursue education against all odds. However, given his family's challenging circumstances, Shetan couldn't fathom how this would be achieved. He pondered whether this hardship would ever relent. Lost in his thoughts, he walked absentmindedly, not paying attention to the road or his usual hunting activities. Despite the circumstances, Shetan never left without his beloved catapult, preferring even solitude on the farm to going without it.

He only realised he was near their farm when he encountered a cobra while climbing the rocks on his way. Snakes were a common sight in that environment, as the rocky terrain served as a haven for various species. They were often seen basking in the sun, scurrying into holes upon sensing human presence. However, this encounter was different. Instead of hastily retreating, the cobra stared at Shetan for about forty-five seconds with a pitiful gaze, shaking its head and, upon seeing him brandish a catapult, displayed its fangs, hissing in disappointment before finally slithering under the rocks. Shetan, bewildered by this unusual interaction, couldn't bring himself to hunt the snake. He couldn't understand how a reptile could look at him with such pity when it didn't know why he was coming to the farm.

After standing still for a few moments to see if the snake would reappear, he continued toward the farm. As he moved a few yards further, he hit his left big toe against a stone. This heightened his fear, as such an incident was believed to be a bad omen. Despite the pain, Shetan didn't cry-it seemed he had exhausted all his tears, as none came down his cheek. Resolving to face whatever lay ahead, he braced himself, accepting it as part of his destiny.

Chapter Four: Echoes of Disappointments

Arriving at the farm, Shetan found his father gathering firewood to cook. He was about to cut the firewood he held in his hands with a cutlass when he heard someone sneeze.

"Is that you, Baba Emma?" he inquired, initially mistaking the figure for his neighbour. However, as he lifted his gaze to confirm, he realised it was his son, drenched in sweat as he approached the hut. He held the cutlass still mid-air and did not know when the cutlass fell from his hand. His countenance revealed he understood Shetan's mission.

"Burotah ita," Shetan prostrated to greet his father in their language.

"Why did you come to the farm so early today?" his father asked, concealing his surging emotions even though he knew the reason well.

Shetan recounted the day's events, including the humiliation from the principal, and to add credibility to his story, he pulled off his shirt, revealing the furrows left by the flogging to his father, who listened attentively in silence. At the end of the story, his father simply sighed and instructed him to set the fire for cooking.

"I have already put some cocoyam in the clay pot; you can add some more." He then took his hoe and returned to work.

Shetan proceeded with his chores, trying to decipher his father's uncharacteristic silence. Cooking on the farm was nothing new to him. It was one of the things he loved doing as it saved him the stress of rigorous weeding with the hoe, which he hated so much. At such times, while waiting for the food to cook, he hunted birds on nearby trees within the vicinity while keeping an eye on the cooking. He dared not go too far away since he had to ensure the firewood kept burning under the clay pot. But on this occasion, birds were hopping about on the trees close to the hut, but he remained indifferent.

"Could it be that his father would give him the money as soon as they got home, so that he could return to school the following day?" he asked himself. "But if that is true, why must he wait until his second son is disgraced and sent out of school before paying the fees?"

One thing that baffled Shetan was that his father hardly kept quiet on sensitive issues; whenever he did, one could expect the worst. They ate in the usual quiet mood. This was the norm, as Mr Agbaje rarely had any conversation with his children apart from giving them instructions on what to do. The only knowledge Shetan has of his lineage comes from the stories his mother told him.

As soon as Mr Agbaje finished the fourth cocoyam, he left for the back of the hut, where he usually took his siesta. This was where he napped after each meal on the farm, and if the weather was too hot, he could sleep for up to three hours under the tree. He enjoyed this so much, and Shetan usually wondered how easily it was for his father to start snoring barely five minutes after lying on his back on the banana leaves used as a mat.

However, this time around, Shetan could not hear his father's snore; even after about thirty minutes, he was left alone in the hut. Out of curiosity, he decided to peep to see if the man was asleep. He saw his father resting his back against the mango tree, gazing towards the sky, to his amazement. It was then that it became clear to him what his father's silence about two hours ago meant!

After finishing his fourth cocoyam, Shetan could not eat more. He could eat nine or ten on a typical day, but he had lost his appetite this time around. He took his hoe from the hut and headed towards the cassava plantation. This was where he worked every Saturday, and he had about four more Saturdays to finish this section before moving to the cocoyam plantation. But now that he had to devote all his time to farming, he should be able to finish it in less than a week!

When it was getting dark, Shetan heard his father clear his throat twice; he knew the next thing would be calling him to let him know it was home time. All the children were very familiar with this. He packed the remaining cooked cocoyam into a small sack and headed home.

He walked so fast as if he had left a baby that needed to be breastfed at home. His heart was pounding as he descended the hills, mostly when he got to the spot where he saw the snake earlier in the day.

When he got home, his mother asked, "What did your father say after narrating your ordeal?"

"He said nothing, Iyan", as they mostly called their mother in their local language.

My story only met silence." Shetan told her.

She looked at her son and shook her head. It was three hours later that Shetan came to realise the correlation between the pitiful way the snake regarded him, his father's silence earlier on in the farm and the way his mum shook her head.

"Shetan," his father called him from the front of the house, where he was relaxing after eating the pounded yam he had been served for supper. He rushed straight to where his parents sat, his heart pounding heavily. He had been expecting the call, so he was not surprised when he heard his name. However, he knew the moment had come for him to learn his fate.

Shetan stood before his parents in the soft glow of the evening light, feeling a mixture of nervousness and apprehension. His father sat on his wool chair, absentmindedly playing with his snuff case, while his mother, her expression marked with concern, occupied a chair beside him. The weight of the impending conversation disrupted the serene atmosphere of the evening.

Not sure where to start, Mr Agbaje cleared his throat again and opened the snuff case. Though it was dark outside, the *shakabula* placed in the passage provided enough illumination for the family to find their way around the house. Shetan could still see the disappointment written on his father's face. He looked in his mother's direction and could feel the pain she bore inside her.

The second wife was peeping from the window of her room to eavesdrop on their conversation. Shetan was just two years and a few months old when his father suddenly brought the "new bride" into the house from his trip to their hometown without informing his first wife. The last day the family experienced peace and progress was the day before Olayemi was brought into the house, and ever since her arrival, things had been deteriorating. As Shetan grew up, he wondered why his father decided to bring such a wicked woman into their peaceful home!

"Well," his father began, his voice tinged with emotion as he cleared his nose with the back of his hand, "It's never been my intention to see any of you suffer. Since the moment I couldn't advance beyond standard six, I've held onto the dream that at least all my sons would complete what you now call secondary school. That's why I've worked so hard to make that dream a reality. Your elder brother didn't struggle as much to complete his secondary school because of the free education system in place." He paused, his thumb hitting the cover of the snuff case, a gesture that heightened Shetan's apprehension. Glancing towards his mother, Shetan noticed her wiping her face with the tip of her wrapper, a silent display of her own emotions.

"As you are aware," his father continued, "the military taking over all the states did not help situations at all, and since they introduced fees at all levels, it has been difficult for me to pay your school fees. I never even knew that you could come this far, and I think you have seen how difficult things have become for the entire family on a daily basis." He paused once again, opened the snuff case, and used the back of his thumb to insert some into his left nostril.

Shetan, still standing to hear the final judgment, wondered if the old man sitting right in front of him was not to blame for the poverty that had befallen the family ever since he brought in the second wife.

"Since the moment you came to meet me on the farm," his father continued, his voice heavy with regret, "I have been racking my brain trying to figure out how to raise the money to pay your fees, but I have not been able to come up with anything. It pains me deeply to say this, but I want you to understand that you may not be able to continue your studies. There is simply no means for me to raise the money," he concluded, his words weighed down by the harsh reality of their situation."

Mr Agbaje paused to see his son's reaction.

Shetan glanced towards his mother and noticed she was still in tears; her sorrow palpable despite being informed of the decision earlier. Mr Agbaje couldn't help but feel surprised by her reaction, expecting her to have already processed the news. Meanwhile, the second wife, who had been eavesdropping, let out a chuckle, seemingly approving of Mr. Agbaje's words. Her reaction added another layer of tension to the already fraught atmosphere, accentuating the divide between the family members.

Dejected, Shetan retreated indoors, his emotions overwhelming him as tears flowed freely down his cheeks. He felt as though a heavy blow had struck him; his heart was weighed down by the crushing disappointment of his father's words. Meanwhile, Titilayo and Omolade hurried to their mother's room, eager to uncover the reason behind Shetan's distress. Shetan could hear their laughter echoing through the house as they disappeared behind closed doors. Anger simmered within him at the thought of being the subject of their amusement, but he managed to restrain himself from confronting them. After all, both girls were primary school dropouts, and he doubted they could understand the depth of his pain.

Chapter Five: The Struggles

As soon as the children caught wind of their father's sombre mood, they sought solace in their mothers' chambers, each retreating to their own haven. While Shetan and his brothers silently retrieved their tarpaulin and settled into their sleeping spot, the echoes of joyous laughter emanated from the other woman's room, starkly contrasting the solemn atmosphere pervading their own.

Mr Agbaje went inside to sleep earlier than usual; the second wife was about to join him in bed when he turned and said with a sombre voice, "I want to be alone."

She stood frozen in place, her gaze fixed upon him with an intensity that seemed to pierce through the very fabric of the night. The air was heavy with the fragrance of herbs, a subtle reminder of her meticulous preparations throughout the evening in anticipation of this moment. Wrapped in a single cloth tied loosely around her chest, her figure swayed gently, the fabric offering a tantalizing glimpse of the curves beneath. Like two ripe pomegranates, her presence exuded an irresistible allure, beckoning him closer with an unspoken invitation that hung between them, laden with promise and desire.

"Why?" She asked, clearing her throat. But he gave no reply.

Perplexed, she pressed on. "Is it not my turn? Why will I not accompany you tonight?"

Her trembling voice revealed the depth of her dismay at his gesture as she returned to her room.

In that instant, Mama Enitan sensed Mr Agbaje's inner turmoil, yet she grasped the futility of his efforts to make Shetan continue his education.

Mr Agbaje could not sleep throughout the night; he rolled from one end to the other on his grass-made double mattress, which was placed on a wooden bed he made by himself. He could not understand why nature was so partial to him. He desired a change and thought that the lives of his children would at least be better than his, but he wondered if that would ever happen in his lifetime. Now and then, he sighed intermittently in a way that the first wife could hear him in her room. He could not bear putting his back on the mattress any longer as he became uncomfortable with his sleep. He stood up to stretch and sat back on the wooden bed with his back against the wall. It was always pitch-dark in the room once he put out the lantern whenever he wanted to sleep.

"But when on earth will poverty end in his lineage? For how long will he continue to live in abject poverty?" He asked himself.

It was indeed a long night, but alas, the first cock crowed, and he got up to prepare for the church morning prayer. He waited patiently to hear the hourly toll of the bell at CRIN (Cocoa Research Institute of Nigeria office) staff, which is at the centre of the village. The security men of the research institute hit an iron rod against a lorry wheel, which they specially hung from a tree beside the gate every hour from 10 pm to 5 am. The bell could be heard as far as a one-mile radius and served as one of the ways the people of Ayetoro and its environs marked time. However, there were times when the men would fall asleep and forget to do so every hour. He arrived at church when the catechist was about to open the church door, and within a few minutes, some other church members joined them.

"Baba wa tin be ni orun ka bowo fun oruko re ki ijoba rede……" Mr Agbaje continued reading the Lord's Prayer in Yoruba, and the members recited the other part. Every Friday morning, the Catholic Church in Ayetoro had a morning prayer. Apart from making the announcement every Sunday during the Mass, Mr Agbaje was the one who led the morning prayers, which he read out from the Catholic prayer book. This earned him the accolade *"Baba adura owuro,"* meaning the 'father of morning prayer.'

Despite a sleepless night, Mr Agbaje could still recite the morning devotion without anyone noticing the horror he passed through at night. Friday Mass usually started at 5 am and lasted forty-five minutes to an hour.

As the catechist finished the Morning Prayer and the congregation began to disperse, Shetan noticed his father speaking with the catechist. His curiosity piqued; he wondered if their conversation was about his school fees. Though he couldn't hear their words, he saw the catechist shake his head in disapproval. From that gesture alone, Shetan sensed that whatever his father had discussed, the response was certainly not favorable. He quietly walked home to go and get ready for the farm.

This time, Shetan left home for the farm without his catapult. It was the first time in months he hadn't taken it along. It wasn't that he had forgotten; rather, he felt so weighed down by his new reality that the thought of chasing birds and squirrels seemed meaningless. While his friends were in class, studying, he was left to toil in the fields, and the joy of his old distractions had faded away.

Shetan and his two younger brothers had a routine of hunting birds, rabbits, and squirrels. Armed with simple but effective techniques, they would venture into the forest and cocoa plantations, Shetan always leading the way. With his sharp eye and steady aim, he guided the group, while his younger siblings followed closely, eager to learn from their older brother. Together, they made a formidable team, each member playing a crucial role in their hunt for prey.

He reached the farm faster than he would have if he'd brought his catapult. When he arrived at the small hut his father had built from mud and stones, he took off the shirt he wore to the farm and change to his usual farm regalia, tattered clothes he couldn't wear any longer at home. This was to ensure he had something decent to wear back home. He then took his hoe and vanished into the cassava plantation.

Mr Agbaje had a daily routine each time he got to the farm. After checking some of his traps along the way to the hut, he would drop his *shaka-shaka* bag to check other traps set further in the forest for bigger animals. In total, Mr Agbaje had about sixteen traps of different sizes. Each was set along the footpath that the animals had created, and he dared not make the mistake of setting one meant for a rabbit on the part of an antelope!

It was a good day for Mr Agbaje as two of his traps caught grass cutters. As soon as he returned to the hut with the animals, he called out, "Shetan!"

"Yes, Ita!" He answered, a little puzzled by his father's excited tone.

"Come and roast these animals so I can prepare them for drying on the fire." He proudly presented the two prized games to Shetan, who received them with a bow.

When Shetan saw the two animals, he knew straight away that he had little weeding to do for the day. Every time they caught an animal, it was customary for them to eat pounded yam on the farm, which took up most of the day. Shetan had just finished roasting the first one when he heard school drums. The words of their songs floated into his heart like an enchantment; he was caught between his work and the melody of the pupils.

"We shall overcome!
We shall overcome someday!
Deep in my heart!
I do believe!
We shall overcome someday!"

This reminded him of the world beyond the farm's confines and beckoned him back to reality. Established in the 1950s by the Anglican Church, Our Saviour's Primary School was the school for all the children in Ayetoro and surrounding villages. Each morning, students in blue khaki uniforms—boys in shorts and girls in gowns—gathered at 7:45 a.m. on the assembly ground. For about 20 minutes, they sang and clapped in unison before performing the national anthem. After the headmaster's announcements, they lined up and filed into their respective classes.

The school had a drum set consisting of two small drums and one large one, used during their daily morning routine. As a missionary school established by the CMS, the students sang Christian hymns each morning, accompanied by the drums, and repeated the same ritual when school ended at 2:30 p.m.

Roasting the second grasscutter was faster than the first one as the fire was already in an advanced stage. After washing the two grasscutters, Shetan called his father.

"Itah, the grass cutters are ready to be dissected.

"Get me the knife and bring a bigger bowl for me to put them in," Mr Agbaje instructed.

"This one is massive," Shetan observed.

"Yes," his father replied, adjusting himself to sit astride the bowl.

"Which of the traps caught this one?" he asked again, wiping the sweat off his face.

"It was the trap I set two days ago by that cassava beside the *orumu* tree," his father replied.

"Oh, I know the trap you are talking about," Shetan retorted. "That was really fast; it was as if the grass cutter was waiting for you to set the trap and then just walked straight into it." He yawned as he stretched.

"Just walked straight into it…" echoed in Mr. Agbaje's mind, triggering memories of his initial encounter with Olayemi and the unexpected rendezvous that ensued, leading him to his current predicament.

Slightly drunk of the Ososo *Pito* on the first evening of the burial of Okosukho in Okhe, he discreetly made his way home to where he was putting up in Yola to avoid any embarrassment. He saw a young lady gracefully balancing a large jar of palm wine atop her head along the path. Despite the weight, she walked with measured strides, her hands swinging casually by her side as if bearing nothing at all. The mesmerising sway of her figure captivated him, causing him to swallow hard with each step. Though her sleeveless brown blouse showed signs of wear, it remained impeccably neat, tucked into a wrapper weathered by time. Yet, it was her aura of confidence that truly astounded him.

As she approached, his gaze remained fixed upon her until they were mere inches apart. Then, she stumbled, her footing faltering as she navigated a hollow portion of the road. In her effort to save the jar of wine, she neglected her own safety. Acting swiftly, Mr Agbaje caught the jar mid-air, ensuring its safe descent.

"Are you sure you're ok?"

"Yes, sir." She nodded, "I have to be on my way now. My employer will soon start looking for me." She walked over to lift the jar back to her head when Mr Agbaje, who at this time was already carried away by her beauty, offered to help. Lifting the jar, the woman tilted it slightly to receive the load. Observing her features up close, Mr. Agbaje was utterly captivated by what he saw.

"Is where you're going far from here? I don't mind seeing you to the place to prevent any eventuality."

"Never mind, sir, where I'm going is just around the corner. You've done so much for me already."

"It's nothing. Let's get going." He just wanted to find out the woman's place. On getting there, it turned out to be a local bar. They offered him some wine in appreciation. On the way, they had introduced themselves to each other. Mr. Agbaje lingered in the bar, and time passed quickly; before he could realize it, it was too late to leave. But that night was an unforgettable one: Olayemi's care, her tenderness, the feel of her body, her reactions and her gentle demeanour could only be described as bewitching.

"She gave me what my heart yearned for, and I offered her what she wanted." He sighed, "Now, who trapped whom? Did either of us walk into the trap, or did the bait take us?" These questions remained unanswered in Agbaje's heart.

Mr Agbaje started dissecting the first one by placing its back on a fresh banana leaf; he used the knife to dismantle the forelegs and hind legs from the animal's trunk. This allowed him to bring out all the intestines and other things in the grasscutter. He placed them in one of the calabash bowls. He did the same to the second grass cutter, and like a doctor in a surgery room, he carefully removed the little green '*belubelu*' located beside the heart.

"This little thing you're seeing can make all this meat bitter if it bursts and a drop touches any part of it," he said, as he showed it to his son.

Shetan wondered how such a tiny green liquid could cause such devastating damage. He carefully collected both from his father and threw them far into the bush.

Shetan knew the next thing to do. While his father dissected the remaining part of the animals, Shetan cleaned up the intestines by removing all the faeces and making sure they were properly washed. Cleaning the intestines of smaller animals was not what Shetan liked doing, but he still preferred it to weeding the grass. This was because he must take extra care to get all the faeces out of the intestine and wash them properly. The intestines, along with other smaller parts his father cut from the main part of the animals, would be used to make soup on the farm.

Although the cooking process could be so tedious, Shetan enjoyed it more than anything else. The season also determined how easy or tedious it could be. It was much more challenging to set a fire during the rainy season as the firewood was usually wet and took extra energy for the fire to catch than during the dry season. He also needed more water for cooking whenever they ate pounded yam on the farm, but this time around, the work would be easier for him as all four calabashes were already filled with water.

Something happened some time ago that could have possibly led to a catastrophe. One hot, sun-drenched afternoon, Shetan had already placed the cocoyam and cassava on the fire when he realised he had forgotten to fetch water on his way to the hut, as his hunting for rodents had taken him through another route. His mind raced for a solution. Baba Emma's cocoa farm wasn't far off, and while the water there was known to be slightly brackish and not the best for drinking, it was better than nothing. Shetan grabbed a calabash, hurriedly filled it at the cocoa farm's water source, and balanced it on his head, determined to return before his father noticed his absence.

But as he rushed back, something strange happened. The path he knew so well began to feel unfamiliar; the trees seemed to close in, and the air felt thick with confusion. Shetan walked faster, but the more he moved, the further he seemed to drift from his farm. After what felt like hours, he realised he was completely lost. He stopped, looked around, and suddenly wondered— "How did I get here?" Shetan muttered under his breath. His mind whirled, but the answer didn't come. He glanced up at the calabash on his head, now feeling absurd. What was he even doing with it?

His mind had been clouded, and he had wandered aimlessly in the bush. With no other option, he poured out the water and set off with the empty calabash, hoping to find his way back. After another half hour of stumbling through the wild, Shetan finally recognised a spot he knew—a hunting ground he and Evans frequented. However, it was five miles away in the opposite direction. Realising he was too far from their farm, he decided to head home instead.

His mother was shocked when she saw Shetan walk into the house through the back door, her eyes wide with surprise at the sight of him—especially with an empty calabash in his hand.

"Shetan?" she asked, her voice a mix of shock and confusion. "What happened? Why are you coming from that direction? And with an empty calabash?"

Shetan sighed, trying to collect his thoughts. "Mama, I don't know. I went to fetch water, but the path... all I know is that I was just walking around trying to find my way, not knowing where I was going."

His mother's face softened in concern; she quickly looked for her slippers and followed him back to the farm.

Meanwhile, at the farm, his father grew increasingly anxious. He had been waiting for Shetan to call him so they could pound the yam together, but time was ticking by, and when he did not hear from his son, he decided to go to the hut. He called out for Shetan, but the only response was the rustling of leaves in the wind. Worried, he rushed to check his four big traps and felt a little relief as there were no signs of his son there. Panic began to creep in.

After a while, Mr Agbaje decided to prepare the pounded yam on his own. As he worked the mortar and pestle, his thoughts were on Shetan, wondering where the boy could have got to. He finished the yam and left it to cool as he sat down, hoping his son would return soon.

Then, after what felt like an eternity, Shetan and his mother appeared at the farm.

Shetan, now visibly shaken, recounted his ordeal to his father.

Mr. Agbaje's face relaxed with relief, though his eyes hardened with understanding. He knew what had happened. Shetan must have stepped on *Obiriko* leaf, a plant known for its mystical and mysterious powers. If someone's skin touched the leaf, they could lose awareness of their surroundings and become disoriented for hours.

Shetan frowned, still puzzled. "But how? How can a leaf make you lose your senses like that? Just by touching it?"

Mr Agbaje nodded slowly, his expression serious. "That leaf is tricky. It has a powerful effect on the body. Once you touch it, it sends you into a state of confusion. You lose your way and forget where you are and what you're doing. It's as if your mind just... shuts off. It's like magic but in nature."

Shetan shook his head in disbelief. "A leaf... making someone forgetful?"

"Yes, just a leaf," his mother replied, her voice soft but firm. "It's a reminder that some things in this world are beyond what we can understand. And you've learned that the hard way today."

That leaf is no joke. You never know when you'll step on it. "It has a way of playing tricks on you," his father added.

Shetan still felt shaken. "So, I wasn't myself all that time? I didn't even know where I was going."

"You were under the plant's spell," his father said, nodding. "But you're back now, and that's what matters."

Shetan glanced at the pounded yam. The meal was ready, but it had lost its warmth, just as his mind had lost its clarity.

"Well," he said with a sheepish smile, "I suppose I'll be more careful about where I step next time."

And his parents, though relieved, could only smile at the lesson learned the hard way. Since that day, Shetan never missed fetching water on his way to the hut.

"Shetan," his father called from inside the hut.

Shetan left the intestines he was cleaning and went to meet his father inside the hut.

"After you've finished washing those items, add them to the ones I've already placed in this clay pot for soup," his father instructed. "Then, gather some pepper, tomatoes, and cassava leaves, grind them together, and pour them into the soup pot."

"Oh, Itah," Shetan replied.

Mr Agbaje checked the meat he placed on the fire once again to ensure that the fire was not too much for them. He took his hoe and went into the yam plantation to work.

Shetan needed not to be told that he should keep a constant eye on the meat so that the fire would not get out of hand. The day went so quickly for Shetan, and he was surprised that he did not even think much about school. He was excited about the quantity of meat and pounded yam he would eat on the farm that day.

Immediately after Shetan washed the intestines, he poured them into the small clay pot and went to the cassava farm to gather some young leaves and other ingredients. When plucking the cassava leaves, he took great care to select the right ones, as there were different species of cassava, and it had to be the one with red stripes on the back. After collecting enough for the soup, he obtained some ripe peppers and tomatoes and quickly returned to the hut. He washed the stone on which they grind the items. The stone had been naturally designed for this purpose. Its hollow shape makes it perfect for a smaller stone to rub against whatever they wish to grind smoothly.

He placed a small quantity of the leaves in the hollow stone and used the smaller rock to rub back and forth until it was smooth. As soon as this was done, he used the large silver spoon to scrape the liquid into the clay pot that contained the meat and repeated the same process until he had finished with the leaves, the pepper and the tomatoes.

He had barely finished the grinding when Mr Agbaje called him.

"Take this cocoyam, get some cassava tubers with it and cook them." Mr Agbaje directed.

Shetan took them into the hut, where he washed the cocoyam, peeled the cassava tubers, and carefully arranged them in the clay pot. He allowed the cocoyam to boil for a while before adding the cassava on top. The sun had reached the centre of the sky, marking midday. With no clock or wristwatch in sight, Mr Agbaje relied on the sun's position to gauge the time, a skill Shetan had intuitively learned from his father.

Returning to the hut, his father placed the soup pot beside the fire, seasoning it with salt and oil before covering it. He instructed Shetan to retrieve the mortar and pestle for pounding. Once the cocoyam and cassava were cooked, Mr Agbaje removed the pot from the fire, replacing it with the soup pot. He positioned the mortar under a nearby tree and directed Shetan to transfer the cocoyams for pounding while he handled the task.

The pounded yam was ready in a matter of minutes, accompanied by a brief wait for the soup. The farm's soup-making process differed from Mama Enitan's at home. Ingredients were added sequentially, and Maggi seasoning was notably absent. Shetan never questioned his father's methods, appreciating the unique and delicious taste of their farm-made soup.

They dined from the same calabash set: one for pounded yam, another for meat, and a third for soup. Mr. Agbaje typically cooked enough soup for the day, as leftovers were rare on the farm. Shetan enjoyed the abundance of meat, especially when the girls stayed home. Yet, despite the feast, Shetan couldn't help but wish they didn't have to come to the farm, fearing there would not be enough food to satisfy everyone.

Shetan cleaned up all the items they used for cooking, including the mortar and the pestle. He was surprised when his father told him to go home with the meat after washing the pots and the calabash bowls. He was happy as he would have time to see his friend, Evans, whom he had not seen since the day he was sent away from school. He learned that Evans had come to check on him twice, but he could not go to his friend's house as it was always dark before returning from the farm.

The journey home was quite a fast one. Despite being in haste, he did not forget to take his bath in the stream; however, this time, he did not use the *irebu nawa* leaf, which would have delayed him further.

His mother was surprised to see him at that time. However, when she saw the grass cutters, she knew her husband had decided to send him home early so that she could use part of the meat to cook soup for dinner.

As soon as he dropped the bag, he changed into his housewear and headed to Evans's house. Getting to his bosom friend's house took him less than two minutes. Evans was preparing *Akpu* when Shetan got there. In a house of five boys without any girl around, Oluchi, the only girl among the six children of Mr Okoro, was sent to their village for secondary school, and she hardly came home, even during the holidays. Some villagers even totally forgot that Mr Okoro had a daughter. Unlike Mr Agbaje, who did not allow his male children to do any domestic work, the boys' duties in Mr Okoro's house were not limited, and they helped their mother with all household activities.

Evans was so happy to see his friend after three days of not seeing each other.

"Are you soon coming back to school?" He asked Shetan excitedly, searching his countenance for some hope.

"I'm afraid I may not see the four walls of the school ever again!" he responded bitterly.

Evans was disappointed to hear what his bosom friend said, so he updated him on activities in the school, particularly the arrogance now displayed by Shonu.

"Can you imagine that tolo-tolo has started boasting that there was no way he would not get first positions in both Mathematics and English this term, now that his rival has been chased out of school?" Evan's pain was evident as he spoke, hissing intermittently.

Shetan felt a deep bitterness in his heart upon hearing the news and wished he could have another chance to teach that arrogant boy a lesson.

After playing with his friend for a while, he announced, "I have to go home now, as I need to rest before heading to the farm tomorrow morning." Shetan smiled at his friend. They shook hands, and he left for his house.

Chapter Six: A Mother's Sacrifice

Mama Enitan pondered her discussion with her husband again and again and felt so sad that her second son, whom he had wished would be able to go to university, had dropped out of school and would now end up becoming a motorcycle mechanic with their neighbour, Pele. The military government had set up a marketing board for farm produce, which caused the prices of cash crops to shoot up in the international market. This boom led to an increase in the purchase of motorcycles by large-scale cocoa farmers, and Pele, as he was fondly called, was the only motorcycle mechanic in the village.

Her husband had told her, "I can no longer make Shetan follow me to the farm. I have no choice but to let him become an apprentice."

With the increasing number of people buying motorcycles, due to the rise in the price of cocoa, Mr Agbaje felt it would be good for Shetan to become a motorcycle mechanic.

"Never…" she told herself. "I will do all I can to ensure he returns to school," she said aloud.

Bimpe rushed to meet her mother to see who she was speaking with, but she was surprised to find there was no one with her in the room. She would soon be leaving the village as she had married a man who lives in Benin and would be departing for her husband's house in a matter of days.

A week after Shetan was chased out of school, Mama Enitan had been busy in their dilapidated kitchen cracking kernels when Fisayo, her second daughter, came in to inform her mother that a visitor was waiting in the parlour to see her. She didn't even notice her daughter's presence as she was lost in thought. Bimpe had to tap her mother twice on the shoulder before Mama Enitan knew that someone was there with her in the kitchen.

"Who could that be?" she asked.

"He said he was from Shetan's school," Bimpe replied.

Mama Enitan sprang up immediately, instructing her daughter to guard the palm kernels from the goats. Then, she adjusted her wrapper and made her way into the parlour to greet the visitor.

"Eka san sa," she warmly greeted the visitor.

"Eka san ma," the visitor reciprocated. "My name is Mr. Adebayo, and I am your son's class teacher," he introduced himself.

"Although the school authority has not sent me here today," he continued, "I felt compelled to visit you personally because of your son, Shetan, who was one of the brightest students in my class. It deeply troubled me to see him sent home, and with barely two and a half weeks until exams, his absence could jeopardise his performance."

Mr. Adebayo paused, glancing around the parlour. Near the entrance to the inner room, a bicycle with two flattened tires leaned against the wall beside two worn wooden chairs. Even the almanacs on the walls were out of date. He couldn't understand how a family could live in such poverty.

"I urge you to do whatever you can to ensure Shetan returns to school," he concluded earnestly.

Without waiting for a response, Mr. Adebayo turned and departed. Despite Mama Enitan's offer of a seat and water, the teacher remained resolute in his departure.

On his way, he wondered why God could give such an intelligent boy to a poor and wretched family!

That message disturbed Mama Enitan, and she told herself she wouldn't give up.

After the evening meal, Shetan was at the back of the house playing with other children from the surrounding area when he heard his mother call him. He went as quickly as he could to the front of the house, where his mother and father were relaxing before going to bed.

"I know you may not expect this, mostly from me, but I have spoken with your father, and he has agreed to release you to me so that we can go to Mama Olu's quarry and carry *pounpoun* to gather money to pay your school fees," his mother said.

Tears of joy welled up in his eyes as they streamed down his cheeks. Overcome with emotion, he immediately prostrated himself in gratitude, thanking his parents for their decision. He promised to care for them in their old age.

Shetan's sleep that night was different as he prayed for the day to break in time so he could start the journey that would see him back at school. The following morning, rather than going with his father to the farm, he waited until his mother was ready, and they both went to Mama Olu's quarry site. The irony was that they would have to pass the road in front of the school to get to the site, but since they left early, no students were in the school compound yet.

Despite the early hour, the mere sight of the school triggered a cascade of emotions within him. He couldn't help but feel a pang of longing as he passed by the school, his gaze lingering on the familiar surroundings. Memories of laughter-filled classrooms and bustling corridors flooded his mind, juxtaposed against the harsh reality of his current situation. The empty school compound served as a poignant reminder of the life he once knew. With each step, Shetan couldn't shake the bittersweet feeling that tugged at his heart, a silent testament to the complex emotions stirred within him as he journeyed towards the quarry site.

As soon as they arrived at the site, they collected two poun-pouns from Mama Olu with a digger, an iron sieve, two hammers, and a cutlass. Every worker's duty was to locate a spot where they could find enough gravel and pebbles, and at times, individuals had to dig deep into the ground with the digger. The workers sieved the sand away from the rocks so it could be clean, and the hammers were used to break any large stones to a specific size and shape so that they wouldn't be too small or too big. These stones were then poured into the poun-poun and carried to a spot Mama Olu had already cleared for it. She recorded each trip made by everyone, and each poun-poun was five kobo. This means they had to go one thousand times to raise the fifty Naira needed for Shetan's school fees.

There were two different spots: one for the gravel and the other for the stones. Whenever it was high enough, Mama Olu would contact her buyers in Alade and Idanre, and they would send tippers to pick them up. Two men usually loaded the tipper with shovels, and it was one of the most demanding jobs Shetan had ever seen!

In the early years of Mama Enitan's work, she would single-handedly carry the poun-poun on her head. However, this task became increasingly difficult for her to manage alone over time. Today, with Shetan's assistance, the burden of lifting became much lighter as they supported each other in the task. When working alone, Mama Enitan devised a method of filling the poun-poun herself: she would place the empty vessel on her head and carefully pour the pebbles or stones into it using a bowl. Yet, this approach posed its own risks, especially when attempting to rise with the heavy load.

Mama Enitan could vividly remember what happened two years ago to Mrs Alonge, whose dream of working in the quarry was dashed due to the spinal injury she suffered when her *poun-poun* fell backwards as she attempted to get up.

To reduce his mother's burden, Shetan told his mother that he would do the lifting while his mother should focus on gathering and sieving the stones.

When the sun got to the centre of the head, Mama Enitan called his son.

"Bring out the garri in the tray and the four-litre container of water we left under the tree," she instructed, "so we can have our lunch."

Tired but determined to carry on till the end of the day, Shetan went to pick up their lunch items. This includes *garri, kuli kuli,* a few palm kernels, two fresh peppers, and a pinch of salt.

As they sat down to eat, Shetan looked at his mother, and tears welled up in his eyes as he observed her tired and worn-out appearance. He couldn't understand why she would push herself so hard, all for his sake.

He could not help the tears flowing down his cheek.

"Iyan", He called his mother.

Mama Enitan, who was quietly soaking her garri while at the same time observing his son, turned to look at him.

"Why didn't you allow me to go and learn motorcycle mechanic rather than putting yourself through this stress," He asked with a mouth full of garri and kuli kuli.

"My son", She responded. "I have to make this sacrifice as you cannot see what I see ahead."

Shetan stood up to look before him to see what his mother was talking about but could only see the trees under the bright sun. His mother, for the first time since they got to the quarry, smiled and said:

"This won't make meaning to you now, but someday, you will come to know the importance of this crucial decision in your life endeavour."

Shetan thanked his mother and promised again that he would do all he could to take good care of her and protect her interests. His mother looked at her promising son and could see his incredible determination. Although Shetan was her second son, the bond between her and Shetan was more robust than that between her first son. This may be because Shetan has lived with her longer than her first son, who was sent to their hometown, Ososo, for his secondary school. Shina also left for Benin to learn technical work after finishing secondary school.

Despite her present predicament, Mama Enitan still strongly believed her dream of seeing at least one of her sons attend a university would someday come to reality in her lifetime!

Mama Enitan was lost in thought as she ate her remaining lunch. She did not even know when the quarry's owner got to where they were having their lunch. What brought her attention back was when her son shouted, "Iyan, Iyan," as she looked towards her son, she saw the woman standing right in front of her.

"Eka san, Mama Olu". She greeted her, and the woman asked why Shetan was not in school that day.

Mama Enitan narrated the whole story to her as she did to many other people who saw them on their way to the quarry site that morning.

Mama Olu left them and walked towards the gravel collection point, but to their amazement, she had not gone more than ten yards when she decided to return to them. Shetan was wondering what could make the woman turn around suddenly.

"From the look of things, it will take more than two weeks or more for you to make fifty Naira to pay this boy's school fees". She paused for a moment before continuing. She must have observed the glitter in the eyes of mother and son. "What if I lend you the money this evening so he can go back to school tomorrow, and you continue to work until you cover the money?" Mam" Olu asked her.

Mama Enitan could not believe the luck that had just shined on her. Although she knew it would be challenging for her, the fact that Shetan would return to school filled her with joy.

"Shetan", Mama Olu called him.

"Come and see me later this evening at home so that I can lend your mother the money for you to go back to school tomorrow". She announced.

Shetan was short of words. He did not know when he prostrated three consecutive times to thank the *angel* God brought their way. Even though the woman had only lent them the money, he knew that he would be back to school to take part in the examination that would be coming up in two weeks.

As soon as the woman left, he packed the bowl of garri he was drinking and told his mother that he was full. His mother could not even continue as well as a result of the joy. They continued their work with his mother saying *"Evesho ogboh oo" every* now and then.

The day went so quickly, and when the sun was setting, his mother told him it was time for them to go home. When they counted how many trips they had made and checked with Mama Olu, Mama Enitan said they had made seven Naira and twenty Kobo.

Unlike her husband, Mama Enitan did not like to stay so late on the farm; besides, she was already tired and still needed to overlook the cooking of the dinner.

On their way home, Mama Enitan expressed her joy that his son would return to school again; he advised him always to be an excellent child so that he could one day go to the university and become a Youth Corper. Shetan laughed when his mother talked about him going to university.

"What's funny about what I said?" She asked tenderly.

"We struggle to pay a common fifty Naira for my secondary school; where will we get hundreds of Naira to cover university expenses?" He asked bluntly.

"My son", she said, "I know my head, and that of my mother will pave the way for that". She prayed.

Shetan grudgingly said, *"Amin,"* but deep down inside him, he could not comprehend how they could raise money to finish his secondary school, and not to talk about going to the university.

As soon as Shetan got home, he broke the good news to Evans. As he was about to enter Evans's room, he saw Mrs Okoro in the corridor preparing the stuff for the next day's village market.

"Shetan, how are you? She asked. "Any news about…"

Shetan cut in abruptly. "Yes, I will be resuming school tomorrow", he gladly told her.

Mrs Okoro was so happy for him. Evans was also delighted when he learned his best friend would return to school the following day. Shetan collected all the notes he had missed from Evans and raced back home to start copying. As soon as he arrived home, his mother told him to go and meet Mama Olu to collect the money from her. He dropped the notebooks and raced to her house.

Mama Olu lived with her husband, who had a Suzuki 120 motorcycle. One thing that baffled Shetan and probably many other children in the village was that the man never untied the white bandage around his left ankle. So many thoughts came to his mind on his way to collect the money from Mama Olu. He could not imagine what would happen if he got there and the woman changed her mind, or if he collected the money and the money mysteriously got lost on his way back home., or "*What if someone robbed me and collected the money from me?*" He asked himself. This made him grip the money even tighter as he raced straight home immediately Mama Olu handed it to him.

Chapter Seven: Victorious Return

All the members of Shetan's class were happy to see him back, and they warmly welcomed him back to the class, except Shonu, whose attitude was glaring at everybody.

Shonu was surprised to see Shetan back at school, but he reasoned that catching up on missed lectures would be nearly impossible, with exams looming in less than two weeks. As Shetan stood on the assembly ground, students from other classes couldn't help but look at him with pity despite knowing he had paid his fees. However, they couldn't help but wonder why he still hadn't acquired a new uniform despite his absence.

It took Shetan three days to complete all the notes he missed during his absence from school. He declined Evans' gesture to help him so that he could finish in time. According to Shetan, "The only way I can meet up with what I have missed in class is to write the notes myself". To facilitate his copying of the notes, he got a separate *shakabula* for himself. Getting the tin and thread for it was not easy, but he was lucky to find a tin at the refuse dump in *Alanjibiti.*

"Why was Shonu behaving that way towards you," Evans asked. "Well, it is evident that he is not happy I am back", Shetan replied.

They laughed over it and went back to their seats.

Preparing for the examination was one of the most challenging things Shetan had ever faced at that stage of his life. However, the examination was easier than he had feared. Although he put in extra effort to ensure he did not view his being away from school as an excuse for underperformance, he never realised he could catch up with his notes within a short time. Besides, he promised his mother that he would give her value for her hard work through the examination result. Despite not having most of the recommended textbooks required for the eight subjects, he borrowed them from Evans and others who cared to lend him their books. Bimbo even lent him her integrated science textbook for three days!

Shetan despised reading with *Shakabula* as the smoke stung his nostrils, but his family's financial constraints meant they couldn't afford more than one ordinary lantern, which was always kept in his father's room. In the village of Ayetoro, despite the local government commissioning electricity, only a handful of residents could afford it at that time. The majority of mud houses relied on lanterns and *Shakabula* for light at night.

Mr Agbaje's house shared a boundary with the Christ Apostolic Church, and most often, the security light at the back of the mission house helped to lighten the frontage of his home. There were times when Shetan would move closer to the church building so that he could read with the fluorescent light. However, that privilege ended when the church erected a high fence around it, which now covered the fluorescent light.

The school had barely finished its exams when news started filtering around that the state government would close it down as part of the military government's efforts to reduce costs and budget. The entire village took the news with great sadness. What started as a rumour became real when the pupils were asked to copy the letter on the blackboard to invite their parents for an urgent PTA meeting with the principal at noon the following Friday.

The letter stated in part that the purpose of the meeting was "to give parents an update on the current government decision so that you can take decisive action on the future of your child(ren), and we implore all parents to be present".

When Shetan got home, he first read the letter in English to his mother, and the mother was expecting him to translate it into their local language, but when she noticed the game his son was trying to play on her, she laughed and said

"Oh, you think I don't understand what you just read in English?" she asked, raising an eyebrow.

Shetan chuckled, his eyes twinkling with mischief. "If you do, then tell me what the letter means."

With that, he laughed again, switching effortlessly into their local dialect as he began to translate it for his mother.

Mama Enitan could not understand why the Buhari/Idiagbon government could be so callous as to plan to close down the only secondary school in the Local Government Headquarters.

The hall was filled to the brim. All the parents were apprehensive when the school principal came out to address them. Mama Enitan represented her husband as she always did in all the parent meetings, even though she did not know how to read or write. She had never missed any of the parent's meetings for her children and those of the second wife. Apart from the market and the places of worship, the parents' meeting served as an avenue for parents to see friends from neighbouring villages that they had not seen for a while. And for whatever reason, most of those attending such gatherings were primarily women. The hall was noisy as the women paired up with their friends to gossip and discuss different issues.

The principal walked into the front of the hall with the vice-principal and some teachers. All the parents in the room stood up to greet them, and no one would ever imagine that the same room that was so noisy just a few minutes ago had suddenly become quiet.

"Good afternoon to you all," the principal greeted the parents. "I am quite certain that most of you will have heard the news that this school will be among those to be closed down by the military government," he bluntly stated.

The parents murmured, and the hall became rowdy once more. People were talking, and some put their hands on their heads, while others looked confused.

The principal called for an order in the hall.

"I believe this is a meeting of adults", he stated, "and I expect you all to behave maturely. I did not bring you here to waste your time", he continued. "This is the last time I will see most of you as the school will be shut down at the end of this third term. I am sure some students will be able to continue their studies in another school, while a few ones like em em.." He swallowed his words as he was about to cite Shetan as an example, "will surely drop out."

He paused as some of the parents grumbled. Most were devastated, and some were even crying!

"We also want to use this opportunity to commend our teachers and other members of staff, who have worked so hard to ensure that we achieve this height," he reiterated. "Moreover," he continued, "we want to use this opportunity to appreciate those students who have excelled in their academic endeavours. I will now call on the vice principal, who will call the names of the best students in the last examination. But before I do that, I want to call into the hall all the students," he concluded.

The principal thanked all the parents and bid them farewell. He reminded the students to be good ambassadors of the school wherever they found themselves and to make him proud in the future. The parents walked home with their children, and so many came to greet Shetan personally for his hard work.

That was the last time Shetan and Shonu were in the same class as his father, who took him back to Akure to further his studies.

Chapter Eight: Owenco

Settling down was not only challenging for Shetan but also tedious, as the new school posed a different challenge. Although Owenco was more extensive in landmass and population than his previous school, Shetan believed that the quality of teaching at his former school surpassed that of the new place. Other smaller schools around the villages were also shut down, making Owenco a destination for most parents in the neighbourhoods who could not send their children to schools in nearby towns such as Akure, Idanre, or Ondo town. Unlike his previous school, which had only two L-shaped blocks, Owenco boasted five long blocks, one big hall, and a workshop built for technical studies, which never saw the light of day as all the technical studies equipment was left to decay!

One thing that made Shetan happy was being in the same class as Evans. In total, twelve of them who were in the same class transferred from their previous school to Owenco. Shetan was surprised that Gbenga decided not to further his studies. What pained him most was that it was Gbenga's slippers he borrowed to take his first-ever group picture in year two, a memory he couldn't shake off.

Despite the school being further away and in another local government area, they had to cross the Ayetoro dam bridge, pass through Owena market, and cross the expressway to get to school.

Mama Enitan never fancied Shetan going to Owenco as crossing the express was a great concern for every parent in the communities.

A jolting incident on the expressway sent shockwaves through the village for weeks. It happened on Owena Market Day amidst the bustling crowd and lively atmosphere. Suddenly, the screech of a car, followed by a loud bang, pierced the air, catching everyone in the market and its vicinity off guard. The noise was so pronounced that even people who were deaf or hard of hearing couldn't feign ignorance. In response, students abandoned their ongoing lessons and hurried towards the gate, eager to see what had happened. However, the principal swiftly intervened, ordering the gate to be locked to prevent the students from pouring out. He then sent a teacher to investigate the cause of the commotion. Tragically, it was revealed that Sallah's mother, the stepmother of one of Shetan's classmates, had been fatally struck by a bus.

"It's a nightmare I wish to wake up from." moaned an eyewitness.

"Imagine being dragged under a speeding bus for over a hundred metres!" Another interjected, wiping her tears.

"It's all these drivers that shuttle from Akure to Lagos," a man added gruffly. "They always wash their eyes with local gin and then put people's lives in unnecessary danger. Just look at how that poor woman's body was torn in pieces!"

The gruesome scene left a lasting impact on the students that they feared taking that route, but the passage of time stabilized things again.

With time, the increase in the price of cocoa products made Shetan's school fees more manageable for Mr Agbaje. Shetan and his brothers helping on the farm made the work easier for their father. They took over the clearing of the cocoa farm, spraying chemicals on the cocoa and maintaining the cash crops. Shetan maintained a close friendship with Evans; they were always in the company of each other on their walk to and from the new school, and life in Ayetoro became more interesting.

Mama Enitan was no longer strict with Shetan, and apart from Shetan behaving more maturely now, he is now taller than his mother, something Mama Enitan found intimidating. The noticeable evidence of maturity in mind and body was there for all to see. This newfound freedom allowed Shetan and Evans to engage in activities their parents shouldn't even know about.

"Guess what happened again yesterday?" Evans asked with mischief in his bright black eyes. Shetan pondered for a while and gave some random answers but failed. "Look, Evans," He said impatiently, "only you can kill this riddle. Unless you tell me, I don't know."

"Arike and I met in the uncompleted building behind my house yesterday evening, and we were almost caught if not for my intuition," Evans revealed in excitement.

Arike was so promiscuous that boys in Ayetoro village nicknamed her "Kinkò" as she never turned down any boy who made advances to her; whether such was older or younger than she was, it did not count; they all received her consent. Like Evans, a year younger, got her approval that they had their rendezvous regularly in the uncompleted building.

"I don't seem to understand, but how do you normally get her attention?" Shetan asked open-mouthed in confusion.

"It is so easy," Evans replied, narrowing his eyes.

Shetan wondered where his friend got such boldness from. He, too, was attracted to some girls in the new school but never had the courage to express his interest.

Shetan's admiration for Sayo was stronger than for the rest of the girls, and he found himself mesmerized by her tall and elegant figure. She was three years younger than him, yet he lacked the courage to approach her.

Sayo's father worked in the water corporation and lived beside the Catholic Church in the village. Whenever she passed by the path behind Shetan's house on her way to the Christ Apostolic Church (CAC) where her family worshipped, Shetan's heart skipped inside him; her black shimmering skin was uncommon for girls of her age in the village at that very instant, he would find himself rooted to the ground without making a move.

One day, Shetan summoned the courage to accost her at the back of their house when the girl was returning from church. He had been watching to see when she would pass, and luckily for him, Sayo was the only one who came for the mid-week service that day.

"I have this letter for you". Shetan babbled and quickly gave Sayo the paper without looking at her face, then rushed back into their mud house. It paid off because, the next day in school, Sayo met him smiling from ear to ear as she handed him a piece of paper. That was how they started exchanging romantic letters.

Sayo was about to move to JSS 3 when Mr Lafe sent her to their hometown, and he was fed up with the reports he had received about his daughter. He even learnt that she was sleeping with teachers, and some senior students passed her from one hand to another. Despite the change of school, Shetan kept close contact with her as they exchanged letters frequently.

Shetan was so happy when he heard Sayo was around for the long-term holiday. Her parents had moved from the water corporation quarters beside the Catholic Church to the CRIN quarters due to their retirement, and Shetan decided to send a letter to her. Lanre came to back to tell him the letter was intercepted by Mr Lafe, who gave him two hot slaps; Shetan was so scared, but luckily for him, the man never reported Shetan to his parents.

Something happened towards the end of their SS2 that made Shetan sad. Evans called him one Tuesday morning before the start of their promotion exams to their final class, saying that he was quitting school to learn a trade.

"But why can't you wait to finish your secondary school?" Shetan asked

"Spend one more year?" Evans screamed, "My dad had already arranged with one of his uncles in Kano, who has agreed that I should come and serve him for six years, after which he will settle me, and I will become my own master," he concluded

Shetan was very sad to hear this. He wondered why the world was so unbalanced. Here was Mr Okoro, who had the money to train his children even up to the university level, but the first son was dropping out of school to learn the trade.

"Why is it that Igbos think only about business and money?" He asked himself.

It was common then among the Igbos in Ayetoro to send their children to learn a trade rather than encouraging them to further their education. However, Shetan thought that Evans would have at least finished his secondary school education before they all departed, but it now dawned on him that he would be left alone. He later learned from Evans that the arrangement had been made when they travelled home the previous Christmas, and he was looking forward to it. Shetan pleaded with Evans, but all his pleading yielded no positive result.

Evans had, among many other things, been protecting him from bullies; he knew he could never have a friend as strong as him again. He was still thinking of life without his best friend when Evans came up with an idea.

"Hey, what about if we travel to Kano together?" Evans retorted.

He has not even allowed Shetan to respond when he chipped in, "See, if we go together, we will become rich within a few years."

Although it sounded tempting to Shetan, knowing his parents would never approve of such a crazy idea, Shetan frankly declined the offer and wished Evans the best of luck.

Evans left at the end of the third term. That fateful morning was one that Shetan never got over until now. On the day of their vacation, Evans told Shetan with a determined look on his face, "I will be going to Kano tomorrow morning." Shetan had a sleepless night because of this and even shared the terrible dream he had with his friend when he went to bid him goodbye. But Evan was so enthusiastic and determined about his journey.

Shetan could not hold back his tears as he watched Evans climbing the back of his father's Honda 175 motorcycle with his bag on his leg as the man took his first son to Akure garage, where Evans was to take a bus to Kano. That was the last time he ever heard of or saw his bosom friend.

Neither Evan's parents nor Shetan knew what had happened to Evans in Kano until now. Initially, whenever Shetan asked after him, his parents would say, "He's okay," but years later, Shetan learned from Oluchi that they had not heard from him for years. His disappearance remained a mystery Shetan wished he could one day unravel.

Adjusting to life without Evans was initially difficult for Shetan. It took him more than three weeks to make new friends, but he still missed the presence of his childhood friend throughout his days in secondary school.

Shetan always longed for their early morning walk to Mrs Okpara's shop, where they took two shots of *ogogoro* and even bought a bottle to take to school. They also bought *Tom-Tom with* which to suppress the smell of the local gin in their mouths.

One day, during lunch break, Evans and Shetan were enjoying themselves in the school bush behind the piggery farm when they were suddenly frozen with fear by the sound of faint footsteps.

"Who could that be?" They asked themselves simultaneously. Turning around, they found it was Mr Segun, their English teacher, and their mouths went dry.

"Don't move an inch! Evans and Shetan! Don't even make the mistake of dropping what you have in your hands."

They were surprised that the teacher sat down to *'enjoy'* the drink with them. From then on, the teacher joined them most of the lunchtime in the bush. All that stopped the day Evans left the school, as he was the one who had been paying for the drinks.

The principal, Mr Akomolede, was a principled man, but he was not mean like Mr Faginte, whom Shetan believed was the most heartless principal in the world; however, his vice, Mr Makinde, was a no-nonsense man. His right hand was so fast to give slaps to any erring student that they wondered how a man's hand could be more rapid than the speed of light. Students preferred being on their knees when talking with him rather than standing up. And all the students knew this about him; he corrected any erring student with a hot slap. Still, Mr Makinde was a kind-hearted man who typically picked up students on his way from Akure to the school in the morning.

Shetan would never forget the day he first rode in the vice principal's light green Peugeot 504 Salon. It was the first time he had ever been in such a beautiful car, and as they drove, he found himself wishing the journey would never end—hoping it would take him far beyond the school.

Shetan had just returned from the farm that morning, where he and his siblings had gone to gather produce for the day's market. He was rushing to school when he heard the horn beeping behind him. He wondered who could be blaring a horn at that time of the morning. He moved away from the road and still heard the horn behind him. He decided to look back and was surprised that it was the vice principal. Fear gripped him as he thought he had committed an offence. He was shocked when the vice principal told him to enter the back of the car.

Shetan fearfully walked towards the glittering Peugeot 504 as the vice principal asked him to open the car door. Although that was the first time Shetan would open a car door, he didn't find it difficult to lift the silver handle. He entered and was amazed to see the clean and perfect interior.

"So you live in Ayetoro?" The vice principal asked.

"Yes, sir, just beside the CAC church". He answered politely.

"I always drop my two daughters at the primary school here every morning so that it is easier for me to pick them up on my way home," the vice principal said

Though short, the journey from the front of Ayetoro Water Corporation to Owenco was the most exciting one that Shetan had ever had. That lift greatly impacted him as he vowed to work hard to buy a Peugeot 504 like the vice principal.

As Shetan entered his final year of secondary school, he reflected on his journey since returning to school with the help of his mother's sacrifices and the kindness of others like Mama Olu. Despite the initial challenges and the bittersweet departure from his old school and friends like Evans, Shetan had managed to maintain his academic performance admirably. While he missed the familiarity of his previous school, he had gradually adjusted to life in the new environment, forging new friendships and navigating the complexities of secondary school life with resilience and determination.

As the third term of SS2 drew to a close, Shetan was bestowed with a newfound responsibility as the Chapel Prefect. Initially appointed as the Furniture prefect, Shetan's dedication and exemplary conduct caught the attention of the school authorities, leading to his selection for a more significant role. The role of Chapel prefect carried with it the responsibility of overseeing the spiritual welfare of the students and ensuring order during the assembly. It was a testament to Shetan's integrity and leadership qualities, showcasing his ability to rise to the occasion and positively impact the school community. With this appointment, Shetan enthusiastically embraced his new role, determined to fulfil his duties with diligence and compassion, embodying the values his family and upbringing instilled in him.

Throughout his final year in secondary school, Shetan was further shaped by the influence of Mr. Bakare, the Economics teacher and the teacher in charge of spirituality. Mr. Bakare's unwavering commitment to upholding high morals and principles often made him a polarising figure among students; some resented his strictness, whilst others admired his integrity. For Shetan, however, Mr. Bakare served as a significant role model, exemplifying the values of honesty, discipline, and compassion. He admired Mr. Bakare's dedication to instilling both academic knowledge and moral guidance in his students, fostering a sense of responsibility and accountability.

Under Mr. Bakare's mentorship, Shetan gained valuable insights into the importance of integrity and ethical conduct, further strengthening his resolve to uphold these principles in his life. Despite criticism and opposition from some quarters, Shetan remained steadfast in his admiration for Mr. Bakare, recognising him as a beacon of moral excellence and a guiding influence in his journey towards personal growth development.

As the final exams approached, Shetan immersed himself in intensive preparations alongside his friends. Together, they formed study groups, pooling their resources and sharing their knowledge to ensure comprehensive coverage of the WAEC syllabus. Late-night study sessions became the norm as they delved into past papers, reviewed vital concepts, and engaged in lively discussions to clarify doubts. Shetan and his friends exchanged study notes, quizzed each other on various topics, and provided mutual support and encouragement to stay focused and motivated. Despite the challenges and pressures of exam preparation, Shetan and his friends remained determined and dedicated, drawing strength from their collective efforts as they worked towards achieving their academic goals. Through their shared commitment and teamwork, they navigated the rigours of exam preparation with resilience and determination, ready to face the challenges ahead with confidence and optimism.

The Yoruba Language was the last subject Shetan wrote. It was one of the compulsory subjects, so the hall was filled to the brim. The students were so happy that they finally finished their papers, which marked the end of secondary school. Shetan could not believe he had finally weathered the storm to finish his secondary education. It was not an easy one for him, but the paper had finally come and gone!

The principal and his vice waited for the supervisor to collate all the answer sheets before addressing the student.

"I want to use this opportunity to thank you all for the orderly manner in which you conducted yourselves throughout the examination period. We are so proud of you and wish you the best in your future endeavours." He concluded with a fatherly smile.

All the students joyfully dispersed and went to their separate homes.

Chapter Nine: Finishing Secondary School

Shetan knew he had nothing else to do for the time being other than help his father on the farm. The students had to wait for the release of their results before knowing what to do next, except for Nkechi and Obigbo, who were already betrothed months before the exam, and their husbands were only waiting for them to finish their exams before whisking them away.

Ayetoro was a village of about ten thousand people, and about eighty-five per cent of the dwellers were non-indigenes who came there principally for farming activities.

Mr Agbaje relocated to Ayetoro with his first wife and five children as things became difficult for him. Although Owo, where he lived, was an urban area, the income from his carpentry work could no longer sustain the family. What compounded the problem was the lack of job satisfaction. He left Ososo after his dream of attending Teacher Training College didn't come to fruition and chose to learn carpentry as a way to make a living.

After their father's death, everything took a sudden turn for him. His elder brother, who had always been so kind and generous, called him one night shortly after the funeral. But this time, his voice was different—cold, and his face was stern.

"I won't be able to sponsor your education," Mr. Agbaje's elder brother declared flatly.

"But, brother..." Mr. Agbaje stammered, confusion evident in his voice. "I don't understand."

"What I'm trying to make you understand," his brother interjected, his tone laced with jealousy, "is that I don't have the means to support you through the teacher training programme anymore."

He searched his elder brother's face for answers with the reflection of light from the hurricane lantern in the room but found none. He wondered why his brother reneged despite having the resources to sponsor him. That was how he ended up learning carpentry in Owo.

Years later, when things were becoming tough for him in Owo, he decided to visit his elder brother in Pepeye Village. When his elder brother told him the prospect of working as a cocoa farmer, he saw it as an opportunity to improve his standard of living and that of his family. He worked on his elder brother's farm for a year before he took up *Alagbashe* for four years, where he was able to raise money to buy his first cocoa farm. He also secured *Ikoshe*, a hilly and mountainous landscape he used for cash crops through a good friend.

Three years after Mr Agbaje relocated to Ayetoro, Mama Enitan became pregnant. As the fateful day of Shetan's birth drew near, Mama Enitan endured a gruelling labour as there was no hospital in Ayetoro. Despite being her fifth child, she couldn't understand why this one was giving her too much pain. Her cries echoed through the mud house her husband built a year earlier. She fought against the relentless tide of pain, and when Mr Agbaje, who took the delivery of the previous children, could not bear it any longer, he decided to rush to meet Mama Dokita, a local midwifery

"Good evening, Mama Dokita."

Mr Agbaje, how are you and your family?

"I am not fine; I need your help. My wife has been in labour for two days now, and things seem not okay with her," He stated

Mama Dokita spent the night there, and yet, the baby refused to come out. Perhaps, in those solitary moments of pre-birth contemplation, it could be that Shetan wanted to change his mind when he realised he would be born into poverty, altering the trajectory laid out by destiny.

However, these contemplations were brief, as the relentless passage of time soon thrust him into the unforgiving grip of reality. For three agonising days, Mama Enitan was in pain. When Mama Dokita realised that Mama Enitan was becoming weak, she contacted Apostle Oluwanifishe, who lived adjacent to Mr Agbaje's house. It was through the steadfast guidance of Apostle Oluwanifishe that Shetan finally emerged into the world. With each cry that pierced the stillness of his prayer room, Apostle Oluwanifishe heralded the arrival of Shetan with a determination that belied his tenderness years.

And so, Shetan embarked upon his journey, bound by the ties of blood and circumstance to the Agbaje family. His path was illuminated by his mother's unwavering faith and the guiding hand of Apostle Oluwanifishe; he stood poised to confront the challenges ahead.

About two years after the birth of Shetan, Mr Agbaje travelled to his hometown, Ososo, for the burial of a relative, returning with a woman by his side. Upon his arrival, all the children and Mama Enitan welcomed him with joy and were glad for his return after a two-week absence. Mama Enitan swiftly retreated to the kitchen, preparing a sumptuous meal of pounded yam and Egunsi soup within an hour.

Mr. Agbaje enjoyed his meal so much that he ate every last bit in his bowl. Even the visitor was impressed and used her fingers to get every last bit from her bowl. Mama Enitan offered her more pounded yam, but she politely declined.

After indulging in the pounded yam, Mr Agbaje summoned his wife to his inner room.

"I want to share something with you," he began, his tone serious. "The woman you saw in the parlour is my new wife. I want you to make her feel at home and treat her kindly."

"But I thought you had gone home for Okosukho's burial. When did you decide to marry a new wife?" Mama Enitan asked, surprised by the unexpected revelation

"Quiet!" Mr. Agbaje's voice thundered. "Are you now trying to dictate how I should live my life?" he scowled, his gaze hard and filled with malice. "If you think this one will leave me the way Ajoke did in Owo, you're sorely mistaken."

Without waiting for her response, Mr. Agbaje turned and left to meet his new bride. The thought of ever raising his hand to her again was unbearable. Recalling his brother's warning, he feared the consequences of another conflict. Given Mama Enitan's harsh attitude toward the new wife, he decided it was best to leave the room and avoid the situation escalating further. And that was how Olayemi became his second wife.

If Ajoke had not left after two months, she would have been the second wife of Mr Agbaje, but she could not stand the poverty in his home.

"Agbaje, I can't pretend," Ajoke stated with a sombre expression. "I can't spend the rest of my life with a wretch like you."

"Please, just have a little patience with me. I assure you, things will improve," he urged, trying to coax her.

"Those words are for the naive and ignorant. You can go find them," she retorted mockingly, grabbing her luggage before walking away without a backward glance, leaving Mr Agbaje bewildered.

The two months she endured were a torment for Mama Enitan, as her husband paid little attention to her. Some members of the community voiced concerns about the blatant favouritism displayed. She had recently given birth to Shina, their first son, when the other woman entered their lives. The following week, Mr Agbaje enrolled her in an apprenticeship programme with a local tailor.

One evening, after serving his meal, Mama Enitan sat quietly in a corner, waiting for her husband to finish eating. The meal passed in silence, and when he was done, not a word of appreciation came from him. His mind seemed lost in distant thoughts, as though she wasn't even there.

"People are talking," Mama Enitan said in a hushed tone.

"About what?" He snapped; his impatience evident.

"Your recent actions," she replied softly.

"Look, woman, I don't have time for beating around the bush. If there's something on your mind, spit it out," he demanded.

"All our neighbours are surprised to see how you left me idle at home since we moved to Owo some years ago while the one you brought last week is already an apprentice," she retorted, her tone tinged with frustration.

"Did I hear you correctly?" he questioned, taken aback.

"But what they're saying is true," Mama Enitan murmured, her voice tinged with clear dissatisfaction.

In no time, harsh words flew between them, escalating into a heated argument that culminated in Mr Agbaje giving her a resounding slap- the first time he had ever raised his hand to his wife.

As the situation became unbearable for Mama Enitan, she sought refuge with Mr Agbaje's elder brother, and reported the sudden change in her husband's behaviour. Knowing Mr. Agbaje to be a reserved and easy-going husband, she was convinced he must be under some spell.

Mr Jide was surprised to see Mama Enitan.

"Burota osunumhe sheshi", She greeted her brother-in-law, who also was like a father to her in their local language.

"Burota", he responded.

"I don't know what has come over my husband. You won't believe what I'm about to tell you now. "I still haven't recovered from the shock." She broke down completely and sobbed.

The day Mr Agbaje raised his hand to slap her was a heart-wrenching experience. "He has never raised his voice on me, talk less of lifting even a finger." She choked as she narrated the whole story to him.

The man was furious.

"What is wrong with my brother? "Is he under a spell or what?" He screamed as he brought out his snuff case. "Even if he is, is that enough reason to throw away our agelong family value?" He fiddled with the snuff case without opening it, and his mind was preoccupied with many thoughts. That his younger brother could treat his wife this way was something unheard of in their family. Although he had no woman with him, he decided not to remarry again Since the fourth woman left his house almost ten years ago.

No one had ever been stopped from taking as many wives as one desired, so long as one had the capacity, but what was unacceptable was battery; under no circumstance should it be tolerated.

The next day, he sent *Ita* Peter, the transporter, to relate a message to his brother to see him as a matter of urgency.

Mr. Agbaje was not surprised to find his wife at his brother's house in Pepeye. He knew that was the reason for the urgent summons. His older brother quickly stepped in to resolve the issue, sternly warning him never to raise his hand to his wife again, under any circumstances.

Thus, recalling his brother's earlier warning and mindful of the potential consequences of another altercation, Mr. Agbaje chose to exit the room instead of engaging with Mama Enitan, opting to prevent the situation from escalating.

Mama Enitan was deeply unhappy with her husband bringing another woman into their once-peaceful home. Given her past experience and the hardship her husband had endured with the family of the previous second wife, she wasn't willing to relive that ordeal. However, she resolved to coexist peacefully with the new bride, not wanting to be seen as malicious. After all, she already had two boys and three girls of her own.

Olayemi, however, had different intentions. The house lost its peace when she brought her belongings into the house. Tensions escalated to the point where Olayemi conspired with Omolewa, a relative of Mr Agbaje residing in a nearby village, to oust Mama Enitan from the house.

Omolewa, a single mother of two boys and two girls, had always harboured animosity towards Mama Enitan. She had hoped Mr Agbaje would marry Omolade, her childhood friend, but she was unhappy when she realised the family chose Mama Enitan due to her peaceful family background.

Mama Enitan quickly sensed the need for caution after their move to Ayetoro, aware that Omolewa lived nearby in the next village. Their encounters were rare, usually limited to brief meetings at Owena market, where Omolewa never missed an opportunity to show her disdain.

Omolewa rejoiced upon hearing of Mr. Agbaje's second marriage. She had taken Olayemi to visit Baba Salami, seeking a charm to make the house unbearable for Mama Enitan, thus forcing her to depart and leaving Omolewa as the sole wife. The herbalist instructed them to return after ten days, but tragically, on the eighth day, Omolewa died under mysterious circumstances, seven months into her pregnancy, halting Olayemi's plan for the time being.

Chapter Ten: Journey to Ososo

Shetan took great pleasure in farm work, relishing the freedom to go and come as he pleased without his father's control. For him, this autonomy served as a means to demonstrate that staying late on the farm was not necessarily synonymous with hard work. He was determined to complete all the tasks on the farm, ensuring that his father had little or nothing to do on the farm. Even at that, he knew Mr Agbaje would never stop going to the farm; he must have one thing or the other to do, even if it was to sleep under the tree.

Shetan immersed himself in daily farm work, diligently tending to the land, and within five weeks, he cleared the two sites and tilled the land for the yam and cassava plantation. His father was so happy with the zeal and determination Shetan put into the work. Still, Mr Agbaje was never the type to praise any of his children in their presence for a job well done.

On the evening of the last Thursday in November, Shetan had just finished his dinner of cassava flour and okro soup and was playing hide-and-seek with his brothers when his mother called him from the front of the house.

My "son," she paused for a second and looked straight into his eyes. "Since you finished your WAEC, I have been thinking of what is next for you; although your father still insists that you go and learn a trade, I told him I do not support that as I want you to further your studies."

"But I'm enjoying my life here in Ayetoro!" Shetan interrupted his mother in surprise. "And where on earth will I start from?" He looked up towards the sky as one searching for answers. Apart from the fact that the government had not released their results, he was unsure what else to do.

As if his mother knew what he was thinking in his mind, she continued in her speech and said, "I have the full conviction within me that the gods of my ancestors will pave the way for you."

Her words had, without doubt, silenced the questions in Shetan's heart. He knew that whenever his mother talked to him this way, she must have decided on something no one could convince her to renege.

"I have already spoken to your father about my plans," she announced, her voice carrying a tone of certainty. "This Christmas, I want you to follow me to Ososo so that you can meet Anako". Her words hung in the air, pregnant with anticipation and the promise of familial connections waiting to be explored.

Shetan's excitement bubbled over, and he leapt to his feet, his eagerness palpable. "Is he the one living in Ibadan?" he inquired eagerly, his voice tinged with anticipation.

"Yes," his mother affirmed with a warm smile. "We shared countless memories together in our youth. I strongly feel that something positive will come from seeing him".

Overwhelmed by gratitude and a sense of purpose, Shetan prostrated in a gesture of respect. "Thank you, Iyan, for all your unwavering support," he murmured earnestly, his words carrying the weight of his commitment. Turning to his father, he repeated his pledge, vowing to strive tirelessly to improve their lives together.

Shetan had never left the village for a holiday until his first term in SS3, when the prospect of a trip to the University Zoo in Ibadan filled him with excitement. When he told his parents about the excursion, he wasn't surprised when his father claimed he had no money. Undeterred, Shetan gathered his savings from hunting and paid for himself.

However, when the school abruptly cancelled the trip and it became clear they weren't going to refund the money, Shetan and a few others, including the senior prefect, decided to riot. They set a date for the protest, only to be shocked when they discovered that the senior prefect had betrayed them. Shetan was one of the four prefects severely punished for their actions, which soured his relationship with the senior prefect for good.

Mr. Anako's residence in Ososo stood as one of the most impressive structures then in the entire village. A magnificent five-bedroom house with two blocks of boys' quarters, featuring a six-room boys' quarter directly behind the main building and an additional four rooms adjacent to it. The expansive compound housed a vast stretch of land adorned with various fruit-bearing trees. Mr. Anako, who commuted from Ibadan to Ososo every weekend or alternate weekends to visit his mother, was held in high regard by the community.

Renowned for his erudition, Mr. Anako spoke impeccable English, endearing him to the villagers who admired his kindness towards everyone.

Shetan and Mama Enitan got Ososo at about 3 pm on the last Friday before Xmas.

He was playing with three other boys in the boy's quarter of Mr Anako when the sound of a horn pierced the air. In a rush of excitement, one of the boys exclaimed, "Uncle has come! Uncle has come!"

All the boys rushed to the gate, where a Blue 504 Peugeot car gracefully drove in. Shetan, with a mix of excitement and apprehension, joined the onlookers who eagerly gathered to welcome the tall, handsome man clad in a clean blue native attire that matched the colour of his car.

Mr Anako went to greet his mother, who was also standing near the kitchen with other women, including Shetan's mother. Shetan could see how his mother looked at Mr Anako in admiration and could quickly figure out what his mother might be thinking about. Like someone having a telepathic conversation, he did not know when he uttered the words loudly, "Yes, Iyan, one day you will also welcome me this way, and people around will look at us in admiration."

Everyone looked in his direction, but no one knew whose son he was.

The driver opened the boot, and the young men took the things from the car. Shetan also helped take some of the stuff into the main building. That was the very first time he had entered such a beautiful house. He marvelled at the arrangement of the living room.

"This is beautiful!" he gasped.

At noon the following day, Mama Enitan called his son, "Shetan, Mr Anako wants to see you."

He left what he was doing immediately and rushed to the main building. Shetan looked at the living room again and was afraid to step on the carpet. He quickly removed his slippers and stood in front of Mr Anako. The latter was still talking with Mama Enitan in their local language. Shetan wondered why his father did not follow in the footsteps of a man he felt was about five years younger than his father. But unlike his father's skin, which had suffered mercilessly from the sun due to his farm work, Mr Anako's skin glowed like a newborn baby's!

"I never knew you had another son besides the one who attended secondary school here in Ososo," Mr. Anako said, looking at Mama Enitan with surprise.

"Yes, I do. In fact, he also has two other younger brothers." She responded.

He then turned to Shetan, who was still looking around the living room with great interest.

"What is your name again......?"

The discussion that afternoon changed the course of his life and destiny.

"I have told your mother," Mr Anako continued, "after Christmas and the New Year, you will have to come back the third weekend in January so that we can go to Ibadan together." He concluded.

Shetan prostrated immediately to thank Mr Anako and promised to be of good behaviour. Mr Anako looked at him again and smiled. As he was about to leave the living room and return to the compound, his excitement vanished when Mr Anako called him back.

"Get me a teaspoon from the kitchen," he asked, his voice calm but firm.

Shetan was confused. He had never heard of a teaspoon before. Yes! This may be surprising, but he hardly had anything to use a teaspoon to eat in Ayetoro, not to mention differentiating among the spoons. He rushed into the kitchen, searching for a 'teaspoon' in every drawer.

"Where is the boy I asked to get me a teaspoon?" Mr. Anako roared from the main building.

Shetan was more confused than ever before. He grabbed one of the spoons in the drawer and sped to give it to his Uncle Anako. His Uncle looked at him in bewilderment.

"Are you deaf?" His Uncle thundered. "I said get me a t-e-a-s-p-o-o-n!"

Shetan rushed back to the kitchen with the tablespoon he was holding. On his way, he continued to ask himself what his uncle meant by *teaspoon* and wondered if tea had its own spoon. Whenever they were fortunate enough to have tea in Ayetoro, mainly when his Bimpe's husband came around for a two to three-day visit, the in-law usually bought a pack of Lipton yellow labels, 450g of Peak Powdered Milk and a packet of St Luis Cube Sugar. That period always served as one of the best moments for Shetan.

Every Sunday morning, his father would ask Mama Enitan to boil two teabags of Lipton on fire and pour it into a clay pot where Mr Agbaje himself would add two spoons of powdered milk and four St Luis Cube Sugar. The remaining powdered milk and tea bags were always locked inside Mr. Agbaje's cupboard in his room, and no one dared go there. This ritual was repeated every Sunday morning until the twenty bags of lipton tea were exhausted. The spoon Mr Agbaje used to eat rice whenever they had the opportunity to, which is mainly during festive times, was the same spoon that was usually used for making tea.

"How come Mr Anako didn't want the same type of spoon for his tea?" He asked himself.

Shetan was fortunate to meet a young lady in the kitchen.

"Moshi," he said. "Uncle asked me to bring a teaspoon for him, and since I am new here, I don't know where they are kept." As he tried to hide his naivety.

Shetan was so embarrassed when the lady opened one of the drawers he had been searching for a 'teaspoon' and gave it to him. He wanted to ask the lady if she had heard his question but raced back to hand it over to his uncle, who had been waiting for the teaspoon.

"So why did it take you so long to get me a teaspoon?" His Uncle asked in a booming voice.

"Sorry, sir, I don't know; we call it a different name in…."

Mr. Anako did not allow him to finish his statement when he snatched the spoon from him and asked him to get out!

That was the first baptism of fire Shetan had, and he needed not to be told that his uncle was not only tough but also a disciplinarian to the core!

Two days after the New Year celebration, Mama Enitan returned to Ayetoro so that Shetan could start preparing for his planned trip back to Ososo. Ita Peter was the only driver who plied the Ayetoro-Ososo route once a week. However, during festive periods, he could go two to three times a week, depending on demand, with each trip lasting a whole day. When Ita Peter sold his truck to buy Urvan E220, the community celebrated due to the reduced trip time and increased efficiency for all his customers.

The journey back to Ayetoro went smoothly until the E220 Urvan Bus suddenly stopped about two miles after they passed the Catholic Pilgrimage Centre in Oka Akoko. Ita Peter came out to open the bonnet, and Shetan wondered how steam could be coming out from the engine.

"The van is overheating, and I'll need to get a mechanic to address the issue," Ita Peter informed the passengers in Ososo language as he walked towards the next village.

They had to sleep in the bush until the mechanic repaired the van the following morning.

When they arrived Ayetoro, Mama Enitan informed her husband about her discussion with Uncle Anako. He was so happy and agreed that Shetan should travel to Ibadan. Thus, when it was a week to the time, Mama Enitan booked a seat for Shetan with Ita Peter to drop him in front of Uncle Anako's house. All these plans Mama Enitan made were kept away from Olayemi and her children. Although she suspected that Shetan travelled for Christmas, she did not know where he travelled with Mama Enitan. Even when she asked Mr Agbaje about Shetan's whereabouts, he only told her that he sent him on an errand. When she persisted in knowing where to, Mr Agbaje warned her to mind her business; it wasn't until their return that she was able to decode that they went to Ososo due to the two new clay pots, Ososo's renowned *okpasa,* and various other items that Mama Enitan brought with her.

Less than a week before Shetan was due to leave Ayetoro, an incident occurred that would have been devastating, as he escaped by a whisker. Shetan went to the cocoa farm to finish clearing the side that didn't have any cocoa trees. The intense heat of the midday sun seemed to penetrate every inch of the landscape, causing the leaves to wilt and the earth to crack under its relentless gaze. He diligently cleared the overgrown undergrowth with each stroke of his machete, entirely focused on the job. As he ventured farther into the dense vegetation, Shetan overlooked the subtle indications of lurking danger beneath his feet. An unsuspecting snake was hiding among the dense foliage, its malevolent presence masked. As Shetan adjusted his position, he felt a subtle change beneath his legs, causing a shiver down his spine. He became paralysed with panic upon fully knowing what was right under his feet. At that moment, time seemed to be still as he struggled with the terrifying awareness that he was standing on a cobra snake!

Shetan was overwhelmed by a sudden feeling of terror, and he screamed loudly, his voice reverberating through the farm. His distress call disrupted the peaceful atmosphere, prompting his father to rush to where he was working.

Mr Agbaje hastily rushed to his son's aid, arriving just in time to confront the dangerous serpent coiled menacingly beneath Shetan's feet. With a single, pinpoint blow from his machete, he confidently and deftly dispatched the formidable foe. Shetan and his father were filled with joy upon the serpent's death, which no longer posed a threat. They scrutinised the scene before them, their pulses continuing to race rapidly after the exhilarating encounter.

Shetan was still scared to go to work the following day; however, since he had made up his mind to reduce the farm's work to the minimum, so that his father had virtually nothing more to do, he summoned the courage and went to Ikoshe, since he had now completed the work in the cocoa farm.

On the last market day before his journey, Shetan bought a Ghana must-go bag, two pairs of Okirika jeans, one pair of trousers, and two shirts from the little money he saved from hunting squirrels.

He was happy that he could post a letter to Sayo to inform her about his impending journey to Ibadan to live with his uncle. He promised to be in touch with her once he knew the address so that they could maintain uninterrupted correspondence by post.

The evening before Shetan's journey to Ososo, his parents called him as they sat outside, receiving fresh air.

"Have you packed everything for your trip to Ososo tomorrow?" Mr. Agbaje inquired.

"Yes, father," Shetan replied. "I even took my catapult."

"Catapult?" Mr. Agbaje asked, perplexed.

"I thought I could hunt squirrels in Ibadan, like here in Ayetoro," Shetan explained.

Mr. Agbaje chuckled. "My son, life in the city is quite different; you won't find any bushes, let alone animals to hunt," he patiently explained.

Shetan went into the house to remove his catapult and told his two younger brothers to take care of it. He wanted to make sure they did not throw the catapult arm away, as the string and leather could easily be replaced.

Olayemi was taken aback when she spotted Shetan striding towards Ita Peter's waiting van that Friday with his new Ghana must-go bag slung over his shoulder. The bus stood ready on the road, its horn impatiently beeping. Initially assuming it was Mama Enitan preparing to travel, Olayemi's confusion deepened as she observed Shetan's attire – a black trouser paired with a crisp white-striped shirt.

She wondered if Shetan was relocating to Ososo. However, she dared not ask him, given their strained relationship, and Olayemi kept her curiosity to herself. Shetan's disdain for Olayemi's treatment of his mother was no secret, evident in their tense interactions. He couldn't help but ponder what life would be for his mother in his absence, realising the significant void his departure would leave for his beloved mother.

Mr Agbaje had already left for the farm when the van arrived. Before setting out, he called Shetan to his room

"I want to let you know that I am so proud of having you as my son; please always know the son of whom you are and never do anything that will implicate you or tarnish my image," he said in a teary voice as he handed Shetan three Ten Naira notes.

Shetan prostrated to thank his father and bid him farewell. He promised to write a letter to him through the Ayetoro post office address, which they usually use to receive letters.

Mama Enitan bid her second son farewell, and the bus zoomed towards Alanjibiti, less than 400 meters from their house. As they reached Alanjibiti junction, Shetan closed his eyes in fear. He still vividly remembered a terrible accident that had occurred at this intersection a few years ago.

He had sneaked out of school with Evans, and they were playing table tennis at Aunty Ajai's place at about noon when they heard a loud bang. A lorry was coming from Akure, and the same type of Urvan he was now travelling in was fully loaded with market women and was on its way from Alade market. The two vehicles collided at the Alanjibiti junction, and all eighteen passengers in the bus, except the driver, who was seen walking towards the wrecked van from behind, lost their lives

"How could a driver disappear from the scene of an accident?" Shetan wondered.

He was later told that the driver used *juju* to get himself out of danger. One could still perceive the smell of human blood in the area for weeks.

Chapter Eleven: The Trip to Ibadan

The journey to Ibadan on the third Sunday in January took longer than Shetan envisaged. He was surprised that the journey took them through Akure, which was less than fifteen miles from Ayetoro. Apart from the fact that the trees were passing them at a higher speed than the van that took him to Ososo, he was also amazed that, despite winding up all the car's windows, the inside was very cold! He sat in the front seat of the blue Peugeot 504 GR Salon while his uncle sat in the owner's corner. There was no discussion in the car except when his uncle directed the driver or cautioned him about excessive speed. Shetan couldn't stop looking at the villages and towns they passed on their way, some of which he had learnt about from history books he read in his primary school days.

At a certain point during the journey, Shetan dozed off and awoke as the car stopped to refuel in Ife. Continuing for another hour, Shetan felt a sense of joy when he spotted a 'Welcome to Ibadan' signpost, realising that the pleasant journey, despite the cold car, was soon coming to an end. The sight of beautiful houses and cars along the road left a lasting impression on him. At that moment, he comprehended his father's assertion about the absence of hunting grounds in the area cities.

The driver made a right turn directly opposite the SS Peter and Paul Seminary, followed by a left to enter Mr Anako's street. After covering about twenty meters, Shetan observed the driver honking the horn in front of a gated house. It became evident to him that the multi-storey building in front of him must be Mr. Anako's residence.

They all alighted from the car, and the young boy who rushed to open the gate bowed to greet Mr Anako.

"You people should bring out everything in the booth, cut all the vegetables, and put them in the freezer." Mr Anako commanded the young boy.

"Yes, sir." The boy replied as his uncle walked up the stairs to his room.

The boy greeted Shetan with a warm welcome, and, in an unexpected turn, the driver introduced him to Dele. Despite the weariness from the long journey, Shetan's determination shone through as he eagerly joined in unloading their belongings from the car, pushing past the fatigue that still lingered in his bones.

They took all the food items to the kitchen, after which Dele carried Mr. Anako's two bags, and Shetan followed with the shoes to his room. Shetan was impressed by the size of Mr. Anako's room and the grandeur of his bed. Descending the staircase, he found himself imagining how a man from his father's village managed to escape the clutches of poverty that had nearly consumed his father.

Dele guided him to the boy's quarters, a room located after the kitchen, where Shetan placed his Ghana must-go bag in a designated corner.

Dele couldn't hide his delight at having some assistance with the household chores. Mr Anako's two wives' relationship was nothing short of tumultuous, with constant discord and a lack of collaboration in managing the home. Dele shouldered the responsibilities of cooking and even going to the Bodija market.

The second wife, from the same village as Mr. Anako, initially expressed a willingness to help with the kitchen chores. However, after a heated argument with the first wife—culminating in a dramatic confrontation that led to a spilled pot of soup—she decided to distance herself from the cooking duties permanently.

It all unfolded one afternoon as Mr. Anako returned home famished, his appetite roaring. Turning to Dele, he requested a meal to quench his hunger. Like a whirlwind, the news swept through the house, reaching the ears of the first wife, who wasted no time in making her presence known in the kitchen. Coincidentally, the second wife, who was downstairs in the living room, also decided to lend a hand to Dele and Shetan as they prepared lunch. However, what followed was a mixture of comedy and force as the two wives engaged in a spirited struggle over who would be honoured to serve the soup to their husband. What had started as a simple task quickly escalated into a battleground of wills, with the pot of soup perilously close to disaster. In a heart-wrenching moment amid the tug-of-war with the long spoon and serving plate, the pot of soup tipped over, spilling its contents onto the floor.

The reverberations of raised voices from the kitchen started to disturb the tranquillity of the house. Initially, Mr Anako brushed it off as typical banter between his two wives, and he carried on dialling a telephone number on his landline in the bedroom. However, as the commotion intensified, he could no longer overlook it. With a concerned look, Mr Anako abruptly terminated the call and hurried downstairs, sensing the gravity of the situation even before he reached the scene. Upon reaching the kitchen, he was met with a sight he had hoped never to witness again: his wives locked in a fierce struggle over a simple task. Both Shetan and Dele looked helpless as they attempted to separate the two women.

"What on earth is going on here?" Mr. Anako exclaimed, his voice cutting through the tension like a knife.

The two wives froze at the sound of his voice, their faces flushed with embarrassment as they reluctantly released their grip on the overturned pot of soup.

"Mr. Anako, it's her fault!" the first wife exclaimed, pointing an accusatory finger at her rival.

"No, it's not! She's the one who started it!" the second wife retorted, her eyes blazing with defiance.

Mr. Anako sighed heavily, his frustration evident as he surveyed the mess before him.

"Enough!" he said sternly, his voice commanding attention. "This behaviour is unacceptable. Do you not realise that our neighbours can hear every word you shout at each other? Have you no sense of decency?"

Both wives hung their heads in shame, unable to meet his gaze as he continued, his voice tinged with disappointment. "How many times must we go through this before you realise that your constant bickering only serves to disgrace yourselves and our family?"

As he spoke, memories flooded Mr Anako's mind - memories of the day he defied his family to marry his first wife, of her unwavering support despite their struggles with infertility, and of the pressure he faced to take a second wife.

With a heavy heart, Mr. Anako turned and ascended the stairs, leaving his wives to contemplate his words in the wake of their latest fracas.

Not knowing what to do next, he picked up his car key and stormed out of the house in a state of anger, feeling intense shame that was akin to burning hot coal. As he drove towards his office on Iwo Road, his thoughts wandered back to the inception of his intricate adventure in matrimony. Mr Anako obtained his Master's in Business Administration from the University of Lagos. Subsequently, he got a highly esteemed role as the Regional Manager of Nigerian Breweries in Eastern Nigeria, with his office located in Enugu.

On a significant day at work, he interceded in a dispute between the receptionist and a young woman. Impressed by her composure and resolve, Mr. Anako invited her into his office; that was how they became fond of each other. Shortly after that, she began frequenting his residence in Enugu, preparing meals for him and bringing him much happiness.

Although they were initially happy, their relationship encountered a significant challenge when Mr Anako decided to introduce her to his family in Ososo. The mother was delighted that her son finally brought a wife home. The following day, the woman decided to visit the local herbalist in Ekpe, which changed her perception of the young lady her son had brought home.

Hearing that the light-skinned lady was an Ogbanje did not come as a shock to her because of the lady's skin colour; however, being told that the lady would be infertile saddened the woman. When the revered herbalist informed her that there was no solution to the young lady's infertility due to a scuffle she had with an old woman who cursed her, Mr Anako's mother felt the need to save his son from the impending doom.

Mr. Anako could still vividly recall his mother's staunch opposition to the marriage, the bitter dispute that ensued between them, and how he had distanced himself from her for over a year, alongside his beloved companion, resolute in his determination to undermine the herbalist's claims and prove him wrong.

Over the course of many years, despite their deep affection and unwavering commitment, the couple was unable to conceive a child. Due to increasing pressure from his mother and being influenced by the herbalist, Mr. Anako unwillingly decided to marry a second wife. The choice provided momentary respite as the new spouse from Ososo promptly became pregnant within three months, a marriage that produced two boys and a girl.

The second wife was kept in the village, based on the advice of the seer, until she was almost due to give birth to her second child. When Mr. Anako could no longer bear the weight of guilt for keeping the second wife away from the first, he knew it was time to confront the painful truth. One evening, as they sat down for dinner, Mr. Anako broached the delicate topic with his first wife. The atmosphere was tense as he recounted the years of familial expectations and the subsequent births of his children with the second wife.

Though he could sense her frustration and dissatisfaction, Mr Anako earnestly expressed his intention to bring his second wife to Ibadan, seeking understanding and support from his first wife. Her initial reaction was one of disbelief and anger, a sentiment he understood all too well.

Yet, after a moment of contemplation, his first wife's demeanour softened slightly, her eyes reflecting a mixture of resignation and reluctance. With a heavy sigh, she acquiesced to his request, albeit begrudgingly, understanding the cultural pressures that had compelled him to make such a decision.

And so, with his first wife's reluctant consent, the second wife was brought to their home in Ibadan. Nevertheless, the constant conflict between the two women transformed Mr. Anako's home into a tumultuous battlefield marked by politics, hostility and disharmony. Although he had accomplished great things in his professional life and was delighted when he was transferred back to Ibadan eight years ago, he could not find the serenity and happiness he desired in his personal life since it was overshadowed by deep-seated bitterness and remorse.

Chapter Twelve: Life in the City

Life in the city, it was different, with its busy pace, but Shetan's adjustment was a mix of finding comfort in new conveniences and a bit of longing for the simple things left behind in the village. The complexity of relationships in Mr Anako's family was not new to him, as he had witnessed the same thing happen between his mother and Olayemi while growing up. Still, he wondered how two educated women could be fighting almost on a daily basis.

The daily routine in the house seemed like a perpetual cycle for Shetan. Mornings began with the task of getting the children ready for school and washing the three cars in the house—a Peugeot 504 and two different models of Mazda 323. The flurry of cleaning the cars was then followed by starting the numerous household chores that awaited him and Dele. What struck Shetan as particularly surprising was the rarity of moments for rest, especially during weekends.

Weekends unfolded with a demanding schedule, featuring the arduous task of mopping the entire six-bedroom and two-living room house on Saturdays. They then continued handwashing the clothes the children had used for the week and a trip to the market to purchase necessities for the household. As for Sunday, the only time they have to rest is during the Morning Mass at the Dominican Community in Samonda, Ibadan, and as soon as they get back from the church, they will prepare lunch for the house. Evenings brought another set of responsibilities as they meticulously arranged the items Uncle Anako brought back from his trips. The relentless rhythm of the household left Shetan with a newfound appreciation for the intricacies of domestic life, with weekends offering little respite amid the bustling activities.

One notable challenge Shetan encountered was grappling with conversations in English. In stark contrast to his father's home, where their local dialect and Yoruba dominated communication, Mr. Anako's house imposed a stringent rule: English was the exclusive language allowed. This rule was established to avoid unintentionally offending the first wife, who perpetually suspected that discussions in their local dialect revolved around speaking ill of her.

"So, tell me about life in the village", Dele asked Shetan one afternoon when they were washing clothes at the back of the house.

Dele found himself thoroughly entertained by Shetan's narrative. He marvelled at the tales of village life and Shetan's hunting exploits. The question of why his uncle brought such a rustic boy like Shetan into the bustling city lingered in his mind.

Despite being just a year older than Shetan, Dele had a different educational background. He completed his primary and secondary education in Ikare, a city not too far from Ososo. After finishing secondary school, he moved to live with Mr. Anako, his mother's brother. While Shetan had focused on art subjects during his secondary education, Dele wanted to study medicine. However, he faced a hurdle as he had a P7 in Chemistry and Physics, necessitating a retake of his WAEC exams to meet the JAMB requirements.

After observing Shetan for a few weeks, Mr Anako was convinced that Shetan's proficiency in English would likely pose a significant challenge for him in passing his WAEC exams. One evening, he called Dele and Shetan for a crucial discussion.

"Dele, tomorrow I'd like Shetan to accompany you to register for WAEC lessons," Mr Anako declared.

"Okay, sir." Dele promptly responded.

The directive signalled a significant turning point, underscoring Mr Anako's proactive commitment to guaranteeing Shetan's educational success and his determination to ensure equal treatment of everyone, irrespective of who they are to him. Something Shetan was eternally grateful for, as the development not only showcased Mr Anako's dedication but also opened new possibilities for Shetan's education journey.

The prospect of starting extramural classes filled Shetan with joy. Every time Dele returned home, sharing stories of the happenings at the lessons, Shetan couldn't help but wish he was a participant in those enriching experiences. The following morning, Mr Anako called Dele to give him the money for Shetan's lessons.

"Make sure you bring the receipt for me." He thundered.

Mr Anako was a highly principled man who loved accountability. Anytime the boys needed basic things for themselves, they would list them on a sheet of paper with the cost price for each item, put them

"Hey, Shetan," Dele began, his eyes swiftly surveying the limited selection of clothes that Shetan had unpacked from his Ghana must-go bag. "I can see that only one of your village shirts seems suitable for the extramural lessons."

Shetan nodded subtly, conveying acceptance in his gaze. "Indeed, they seemed like good choices when I purchased them at Owena market."

Dele quickly grasped the challenges Shetan faced in navigating the unfamiliar metropolitan landscape and, sensing his discomfort, made a conscious decision to close the distance between them.

"Don't worry, I know what to do," Dele said, grabbing one of his shirts. "Take this shirt and wear it to the lesson tomorrow. You need to look neat and presentable".

Shetan's eyes dilated in astonishment as he received the shirt. "Thank you, Dele

Deep down in Dele's mind, he gave Shetan one of his shirts to ensure Shetan fitted in. Dele also thought it would be insulting to be associated with a boy who looked unkempt when the girls at the extramural looked at him in admiration

Then, in a surprising twist, Dele said, "You can't look like a village boy and expect any girl to like you!"

Confused, Shetan responded, "Girls? I thought we were going there to learn. Why talk about girls?"

This unexpected turn added a bit of excitement and humour to their conversation.

Dele laughed. "You are indeed a village boy." He snapped.

"Do you want to tell me that you never had a girlfriend when you were in the village?" Dele asked him.

Shetan hesitated before answering. "I used to have a crush on a girl who was three years my junior in secondary school." He stated.

Pius Extramural Centre was in Oba Akinbiyi High School II in Mokola, Ibadan, and it was one of the most famous centres for WAEC and JAMB Classes. Mr Pius, a renowned educationalist, ensured that seasoned teachers were recruited and the students' yearly performance gave the centre a high rating.

While heading to the centre, Shetan shared his admiration for Sayo with Dele. He explained how he always found ways to see her, recounting the day Sayo's father caught his younger brother delivering a love letter to her and how he gave the poor boy three hot slaps. Later that evening, back home, Shetan showed Dele some of the letters Sayo had written to him, and they both shared a laugh over the memories.

Shetan had barely lived in Ibadan for a year when he received a distressing letter through the post from Akanbi, his younger brother in Ayetoro, that prompted him to rush home without informing Mr Anako. His mother had asked his third son to send the letter detailing the challenges she was facing at the hands of Olayemi, and the threat to her life was becoming unbearable.

Shetan could not understand why his father had not intervened. He confided in Dele about his plan to quickly visit his parents, assuring he would return the next day. Luckily for him, it was a Friday, and Mr Anako was planning to travel for a wedding in Benin, where he would go to Ososo to see his mother.

Shetan went to the park to catch the 5:30 am bus going from Iwo Road to Idanre via Ayetoro, and by 8:30 am, he was already in Ayetoro.

Although Mama Enitan was happy to see his son after a year, she was so surprised that Shetan did not give prior notice before coming.

"You didn't tell me you were coming?" She asked.

"Do I need permission to return to my father's house, again?" He jokingly replied.

He hadn't expected to find his father at home at that time of day, as he should have already been at the farm.

After dropping his bag in his father's room, Shetan decided to visit Evans' house to check on his mother and inquire about Evans. To his shock, he learned that no one had heard from Evans in the past year. This revelation heightened Shetan's concern, which is evident in the worried expression on Mrs. Okoro's face.

Shetan's anxiety deepened when he heard about a recent fight in Kano, resulting in the death of some Igbos. *"I hope Evans was not among those killed,"* he muttered to himself, expressing his heartfelt worry.

Shetan gave Mrs Okoro the bread he had brought for her from Ibadan, and the woman was so happy to see Shetan. On his way back home, his mind was burdened with thoughts about Evans and the uncertainties surrounding his friend's whereabouts and well-being.

Mr. Agbaje was glad to hear that Shetan was doing well in Ibadan, but he still couldn't understand why Shetan had come and was planning to leave the following day. At first, Olayemi had thought Shetan was back in the village for good, but she quickly dismissed the idea when she saw him enter the house with only a small bag.

Just as Shetan was about to step outside to brush his teeth the following morning, his mother beckoned him into her room. Mama Enitan began recounting the challenges she had been facing with Olayemi.

"So, she hasn't stopped harassing you?" Shetan inquired.

"Stopped?" Mama Enitan's voice began to crack. "It's as if she saw your leaving the house as an opportunity to escalate her troubles. I thought the passing of Omolewa would deter her from such superstitious acts, but it seems to have only strengthened her resolve to harm me. However, I know the gods of my ancestors won't make her succeed".

Shetan was about to talk when his mother continued.

"Did you know that Baba Salami called me on my way to collect the Church keys from the Catechist last Saturday evening, as it was the turn of St. Theresa's group to sweep the church? He asked me what I had done to Olayemi to make her hate me so much."

"Really?" Shetan interrupted.

"Yes," his mother replied. "He informed me that Olayemi visited him to concoct a charm she could sprinkle on the floor. Supposedly, if I were to step on it, I would fall ill and die within seven days."

"And is my father aware of all these?" Shetan asked, his emotions simmering within him.

"Hmm, I don't understand your father these days. It's as if he's under her spell," she said. "When I informed him, all he said was that I should continue to pray," she concluded.

In annoyance, Shetan stormed out of his mother's room and barged into Olayemi's room without knocking.

Olayemi was sitting on her wooden bed when Shetan pulled her up from the bed.

"How come you cannot give my mother peace in this house," Shetan asked in annoyance.

The woman looked at him, hissed and was about to sit on her bed when Shetan pulled her back!

"How dare you lay your hands on me like that? Not even that worthless woman you called mother could touch me in such a disgusting manner," she retorted, her eyes blazing with anger like a wounded lioness.

Olayemi did not know when she landed on the floor as the impact of the slap she received from Shetan was too much for her. She stood up and saw herself slumping back to the floor again.

"What audacity do you have to talk about my mother like that in my presence?" Shetan growled as he waded off her daughters, who wanted to stand up for their mother.

Within minutes, a crowd of villagers gathered to calm Shetan down, urging him not to escalate the situation further. However, none dared to approach him, not because Shetan had a bad reputation in the community, but because they knew his anger knew no bounds.

Incidentally, Mr. Agbaje was home that Saturday morning, awaiting the monthly *Yamolowo* meeting before heading to his farm. Resting his arms on the window in his parlour, he felt helpless in the face of the unfolding drama.

Even Mr. Agbaje couldn't fathom why he had brought such a troublesome woman into his peaceful home.

Shetan, undeterred, approached his father in the parlour.

"Ita! Ita!" he called out, demanding his father's attention. Mr. Agbaje, unable to ignore the escalating situation, turned towards his son.

"This woman cannot stay here any longer; you must return her to where she came from, or it will be her corpse that returns," Shetan declared firmly.

Shetan did not wait for his father to respond. Instead, he headed straight to his father's second wife's room and began tossing her belongings out. Mama Enitan pleaded with him to reconsider, urging him to think about what people would say, and the neighbors tried to intervene, begging him to stop. But Shetan was resolute, ignoring their pleas. He even went as far as threatening to set Olayemi on fire if she refused to leave.

Initially considering an intervention, Mr Agbaje's stance changed when he discovered the charms Shetan unearthed under Olayemi's bed. Witnessing the mystical objects, even the villagers retreated, acknowledging the formidable supernatural forces at play as they left one after the other.

As Olayemi packed her belongings and left the house with her children, Shetan departed for Ibadan, delivering a final, stern warning that Olayemi was never to return.

This moment marked the end of years spent under the weight of Olayemi's oppressive presence in the house. Eventually, the room she left behind was repurposed by Shetan's brothers, who turned it into their private room.

Chapter Thirteen: My Travails

Shetan found himself shouldering the majority of the household chores. The dynamics of the house had shifted with Dele's admission into the University of Ibadan, and the mounting responsibilities added an extra layer of challenge to Shetan's already overwhelming circumstances. The ceaseless household chores and the ongoing tension between the two wives made those years feel interminable.

One morning, Shetan had just buckled his belt and was about to leave the house to Mr Anako's new site when he suddenly heard his name.

"Yes, Madam," he responded promptly, ascending the stairs to seek the reason for the summons. Upon reaching the room, he found Madam seated cross-legged on the bed amidst an array of cosmetic items.

"Good morning, Madam," He greeted courteously and waited; when no answer came, he added, "Madam, you called me?"

The first wife, mostly called "Madam", continued polishing her nails totally ignoring him. Her calm, fleshy, smooth face revealed how much pleasure she derived from her leisurely and vain indulgence.

Shetan stood there, utterly disgusted by this kind of behaviour and particularly worried because of his uncle's errand. "Madam, what do you really want me to do? I've been here waiting, and it is a busy day for me." he ventured.

She raised her head slowly, her gaze sweeping over him as though seeing him for the first time. For a moment, she returned to her task, letting the silence linger. Then, breaking it with a voice edged in husky authority, her words heavy with unmistakable weight.

"Listen, you brat." she admonished sharply, her words laden with disdain. "Don't ever open your mouth to talk before me next time when I've not asked you to!"

Shetan swallowed back everything he wanted to say and looked at her with mixed emotions.

""Look over there," she commanded, gesturing toward the heap of clothes piled in the corner. "Pick them up, hand wash them, and make sure they're properly ironed before noon. They're not clothes I'd want to be washed with a washing machine. By the way, even if they are, you should wash them with your hands. After all, what is your work here?"

"But, Madam, Uncle asked me to go to the new building site this morning to do some work." Shetan attempted to explain his uncle's directive to work at the new building site, but Madam's anger flared. "How dare you speak back, you wretched fool?" she scolded, her words stinging like a lash. "Who gave you the gut to instruct me? Oh! You've found the food to eat quickly; you now have the strength to talk, right? You vile son of paupers!" The woman's face darkened.

"Look, Madam, please, I beg you, you can say anything you like to me, but leave my parents out of it!" He looked at the woman, and the murderous aura in his eyes scared her. With a steely resolve, Shetan picked up the clothes and stormed out of the room in a rage. He made up his mind that he had heard enough.

When Mr Anako returned home for his lunch in the afternoon, he was surprised to see Shetan open the door for him.

"I thought I told you to head to the new site and get some work done this morning, didn't I?" he asked, his tone laced with irritation.

"Yes, sir. However, madam requested that I attend to some laundry for her, and I am nearly finished with the task," he responded.

Tired of his chores and frustration, Shetan felt he should have a word with his uncle.

"Sir, I need to speak with you about something important," Shetan stated, his voice steady despite the turmoil brewing within him.

"I want to go back to my parents in the village," Shetan said with tears.

"Will you get out of here immediately?" Mr. Anako, who knew the politics in his house quite well, shouted at him and sent him out of his presence, trivialising the boy's grievance. "Don't tell me you're still a baby! You don't bring grievances during meals. Do you want me to choke while eating? Despite understanding the weight of the household chores bearing down on him, Mr Anako opted not to indulge his emotions.

Later that evening, he called Shetan and soothingly spoke to him.

"Do you truly understand why you're here in my household?" he inquired, scrutinizing the young man's expression.

"Yes, sir," Shetan replied, casting his gaze downward.

"Now, tell me, what is your purpose here?"

"It is for me to diligently pursue my studies, aiming to secure admission into a higher institution," Shetan responded.

"Have you accomplished that yet?" Mr. Anako pressed.

"No, sir," Shetan admitted, blaming himself for his impulsive decision to leave when his uncle hinted at the matter.

"Until you achieve that goal, you're staying put. Is that clear?" Mr Anako's stern demeanour brooked no argument, and he continued, "Focus on passing your exams first so that you can gain admission into the university. What will others think if you return home without university admission after spending three years under my care? I promised your mother I would support you and am pleased with your hard work. Moreover, you've already passed your WAEC; you just need to await your JAMB results. So why not persevere?"

Noticing that Shetan had sobered up, he dismissed him with these words: "You are not a swimmer until you can swim against the tide"

One day, an incident in the living room further fuelled Shetan's resolve to secure admission to a university. Tunde, their neighbour and Dele's coursemate at the University of Ibadan had come to visit. The university had recently declared a strike, prompting students to vacate their hostels for a week to ease tensions over disputes between the administration and the students' union regarding increased tuition fees. Rather than returning home, Dele and four other relatives studying at the same institution chose to stay at Mr Anako's house during the break. The group was engaged in a heated discussion about the strike and their dissatisfaction with the university's decision to shut down operations when Shetan entered the living room.

Having been working in the kitchen, Shetan took a moment to rest and listen to the lively conversation about campus life. He dreamed of someday sharing his own stories about city and university life with the people in the village. Spotting an empty space on the three-seater sofa where Tunde and Dele were relaxing, he moved to sit down between them. However, just as he was about to settle, Tunde abruptly pushed him away.

"Are you blind? How dare you? You're not even afraid. Can't you see that this is a gathering of university students, and you dare to come and sit in our midst," Tunde remarked jestfully, throwing the room into loud laughter.

This remark pierced Shetan like a dagger, triggering memories of the humiliation he endured at the hands of Mr Faginte on the assembly ground. He felt a wave of despair wash over him as if he wished to vanish into thin air. With a heavy heart and leaden steps, he retreated to the kitchen. Recalling his mother's fervent belief that one of her children would become a university graduate, Shetan fought back the tears threatening to spill from his eyes.

"Rather than cower because of these abuses," he thought, "they will make me soar to prove them all wrong someday." With this in mind, he went about his affairs resolutely. He no longer bothered about words, intimidations, or body language; jeers and cheers did not matter to him anymore

The unrelenting stress and escalating pressure seemed unending, taking a toll on his well-being. Yet, deep down in his heart, he believed every passing day brought him closer to the dream shared between him and his mother.

Eventually, the long-awaited dream of gaining admission to the university materialised through the assistance of Aunty Rachael, Mr Anako's half-sister, who played a pivotal role in making it happen after three attempts. The joy of this achievement quickly overshadowed the weariness that had settled in during the four years he spent grappling with the challenges of rectifying his WAEC result and passing JAMB.

When Shetan got the admission letter to study at the University of Ilorin, he felt so fulfilled. The intense happiness flowing through him brightened his whole existence, throwing a dazzling shine on his face. Unbeknownst to him, a formidable expedition awaited him in Ilorin.

Departing from Ibadan that fateful morning, Shetan was filled with eager excitement, anticipating a swift journey to the university and returning home on the same day. Nevertheless, destiny had other intentions. While travelling on the road, they encountered an unforeseen hindrance: traffic congestion between Oyo and Ogbomosho. Initially, they were unaware of the cause.

" Please, Bro, wetin cause this kain traffic?" The bus driver leaned out of the window, his bald head poking out briefly as he sought answers from passing vehicles.

"Na serious accident ooo. Na one 21-seater bus going to Lagos jam a truck, and all the passengers in the bus died, but the bus driver managed to escape..." An oncoming driver offered a grim explanation as they continued on their way.

"Another driver managed to escape again?" Shetan exclaimed in disbelief. The other passengers on the bus turned to him, their expressions a mix of surprise and confusion.

Shetan's stomach churned at the sight before him as they approached the accident scene. Twisted metal and shattered glass littered the road, a grim testament to the violence of the collision. He couldn't fathom how anyone could emerge unharmed from such a devastating wreck.

Shetan didn't arrive at the University of Ilorin mini campus junction until 5 pm. It took him another twenty minutes to locate the Faculty of Business. Shetan quickly examined the list affixed to the board. Every moment seemed like a never-ending period as he scanned the list for his name. As he read each name, his anxiety intensified, and a knot in his gut got tighter.

At last, his gaze fixated on the recognisable configuration of characters forming his name, Feyishetan Agbaje! A sense of relief surged through him, completely dissipating the anxiety that had previously consumed him. An intense feeling of happiness flowed inside him, briefly overriding the exhaustion that burdened him.

However, Shetan's excitement was short-lived, as he soon faced a harsh and sobering reality. He looked at his digital watch and noticed it was 5:48 pm. That was when it dawned on him that it was now late, much beyond the appropriate time for him to start the journey back to Ibadan. As he became aware of the challenging situation he was in, panic overcame him. Unable to afford the bus fare, he could not go to the park.

Consequently, he stood by the roadside, hoping to catch a ride, but none of the cars or buses were willing to go as far as Ibadan. After waiting for two hours, he realised there was no way he could cover the three-hour journey that night. He had no option but to return to the university. The question that arose in his mind was where he would sleep.

As nightfall arrived, the Adewole road became quiet, apart from the green and yellow taxis that ply the busy road. Shetan had no alternative but to accept the fact that he would have to spend the night on campus. The issue of where to sleep burdened his thoughts, overshadowing what should have been a time of jubilation.

Shetan returned to the mini campus and stood outside the Student Union Building, a few meters away from the entrance gate. This bustling hub was alive with activity. Inside, students were gathered, laughing and chatting as they enjoyed its amenities, including shops, restaurants and snooker board.

Looking still confused about what to do or where to go, he suddenly perceived the aroma of stew. That was when he remembered that he had not eaten since morning, apart from the slice of bread and water he drank when he left Ibadan! He dashed into the restaurant and requested a loaf of bread and a bottle of Coca-Cola. As he was eating the bread, his heart began to beat faster. Seeing a group of six young men seated nearby, with ten bottles of Guilder lager beer in front of them and wraps of Indian hemp in their hands, unnerved him. There was nothing to show they were students. They looked more like a group of gangsters.

"Is this how they live life in the university?" He muttered.

He quickly finished the coke and returned the bottle to the seller to collect his change. As he walked out of the restaurant, he saw a young man about his age walking into the restaurant.

"Good evening, please...." The young man did not even allow him to finish his sentence when he rudely interrupted him.

"Please, what? I beg my guy, I no get time for all that nonsense. If you need money, I no get shishi with me. Na so una dey go spend una money for girls and start begging to survive, abi, I resemble your papa?" The young man said, brushing him aside.

"But I'm not asking for money..." Shetan tried to explain when the young man rudely interrupted him again.

"See my guy, if you no comot for my presence, I go land you hot slap!" He shouted.

Undeterred, Shetan quietly cleared off the road for him, walked outside the restaurant into the school clinic adjacent to the restaurant, and saw some young men smoking at the entrance. Despite his previous experience, he approached one of them.

"My guy abeg, where can I spend the night? It's too late for me to return to Ibadan."

Pointing to boys' hostel B Block, he said, "You may be lucky to find empty rooms as not all the rooms have been allocated to students yet. Go there and grab one bed and sleep."

When he saw the hesitant look on Shetan's face, he added after one or two puffs, "Oh boy, e be like say, you never dey ready to sleep o. Nothing dey there. No be just to sleep?"

Since it was getting dark, Shetan had no choice but to walk towards the blocks of hostels to the one with 'B Block' on it. He was lucky to meet another student named Michael, who agreed to accommodate him in one of the empty double bunk single beds in his hostel room.

"Oh boy, which one of the beds am I sleeping on?" Shetan asked, surprised that there was no mattress on the bed. He was shocked when Michael pointed to the empty frame without a mattress.

"My guy, this one na baptism of fire to welcome you into campus; the other bunk bed is for two guys that just went out to get something to eat, while the one below mine has not been allocated, and that is why you have the luck to sleep on it tonight." he retorted.

Chapter Fourteen: A New Dawn in Ilorin.

Shetan was very happy to leave for school at last. Mr Anako was happy for him, too, and within his heart, he knew he had once again been able to impact a life positively. He had the conviction right from the day he agreed with Mama Enitan that Shetan should follow him to Ibadan, that he would be able to do something tangible in his life. Although he knew that the past four years had not been easy for Shetan, mainly with the politics in his own house and divisions between his two wives, he felt Shetan wouldn't regret coming to live with him. After all, he came as a naive boy without WAEC results. Now, he not only had WAEC but also gained admission into one of the most prestigious universities in Nigeria.

Mr Anako reviewed the list Shetan submitted again and called Shetan as he sipped his morning coffee.

"You said the total you need for school fees is one thousand two hundred Naira, and you still have to get accommodation, feeding and other expenditures?" He asked.

"Yes, sir". Shetan replied.

"As you know, things are not going well since I was duped by the Japanese man I sent a consignment of charcoal to, and he refused to pay me." Mr Anako reviewed the list again. "For now, I will give you the money for the school fees and an additional five hundred Naira." He then advised Shetan to contact his parents for additional support.

Shetan prostrated and thanked him for all his support.

"Drop Shetan at Ojoo motor park and ensure he boarded a bus before returning home." Mr. Anako instructed his driver.

"Yes , sir." He replied before driving off. Fortunately, Shetan was the last passenger to enter the bus when he reached the park.

As Shetan embarked on the three-hour journey from Ibadan to Ilorin, he could not help but wonder if there was any day without accidents on the deadly Ibadan-Ilorin Road.

Mr Anako's sister had made arrangements for Shetan to stay with another student from Ososo, Bafe, who was in his 200 level. Bafe, who was older and a year ahead, planned to share the rent with Shetan and Okonkwo, who was also his coursemate. Shetan arrived at Agbooba at about 2:30 pm and did not find it challenging to locate the rented room. Although Bafe was not home when he arrived, he left the key with one of the neighbours.

"Are you the one Bafe was expecting from Ibadan?" the woman asked as Shetan bowed to greet the middle-aged woman.

"Yes, ma"? He replied.

Shetan gathered his documents the following day and headed to the Faculty of Business. To his surprise, he encountered a long queue and learned that he needed to undergo medicals first before proceeding to faculty and departmental registration.

Shetan went through the crowd of students to the university clinic, where he met Wale and Anayo, who were waiting to be attended to by the healthcare officer.

"Hi guys, my name is Shetan. Are you also here for medical registration?" Shetan exclaimed, his voice piercing over the low conversations of the gathering.

Wale turned, displaying a fatigued grin that slightly pulled at the edges of his mouth. "We have been trapped in this queue for an interminable duration."

Anayo concurred, his eyes revealing a trace of weariness. "It is annoying."

They faced the bureaucratic pain of registering together, sharing a strong feeling of companionship. During this process, they exchanged stories about their hometowns and discussed their ambitions for the future. Upon leaving the clinic, their connection had grown stronger, solidified by the intense experiences of university life.

Shetan found the 7 am lecture, which was imposed by Mr Ajayi, to be particularly challenging. He hated the fact that he would need to wake up so early every Tuesday morning to be in class before 7 am.

"Good morning, students. "I think it is important for me to set rules so that you will know that I am not here to play…" Mr. Ajayi roared, causing his voice to reverberate throughout the lecture hall as he laid down the rules and regulations during his first lectures.

Shetan's confusion was further intensified by the puzzling remark made by Mr Afolabi, the Statistics lecturer, who made cryptic allusions and bluntly told the students that he was the "alpha and omega of his course and any student that fails to buy my handout would fail" Every lecture was like embarking on an expedition into unfamiliar terrain, where Shetan grappled with the challenge of orienting himself among a vast expanse of complex mathematics and abstract concepts.

Mr Ogunmola, the Head of the Department (HOD), with his arrogant attitude and sharp comments during the Financial Management class, never failed to amuse Shetan as he introduced an additional level of intricacy to Shetan's academic journey.

Shetan's financial difficulties exacerbated his problems, causing a constant sense of distress in his daily life. This constantly reminded him of the dangerous circumstances caused by his lack of money.

However, in the middle of the darkness, Shetan remained determined. Every day, he gained strength from the steadfast support of his friends and the intense resolve that burned in his heart. With his unwavering determination, Shetan moved on, prepared to face whatever obstacles awaited him on his journey towards realising his aspirations.

During his time at the university, lecturer strikes, which practically always occurred, disrupted the academic routine. The primary grievances revolved around the demand for the reinstatement of dismissed colleagues and calls for salary increments.

By the third year, Shetan had attained a state of stability and had wholly adapted to the lifestyle of the university. His academic achievement was above average, demonstrating his proficiency in the educational setting. However, he would have gotten higher scores if he had followed the norm and provided bribes to certain lecturers, who were renowned for accepting such incentives to inflate students' scores. Some female students had to exchange sexual favours for higher marks. Some disgruntled lecturers even commit these anomalies right in their offices and brag about it among their colleagues.

Shetan firmly committed to never using bribery as a means to get better marks; even if he wanted to, where would he get such money? He was satisfied with the marks he received, even when some did not accurately represent the quality of his responses to exam questions.

In his final year at the University of Ilorin, Shetan faced yet another disruptive strike, which began during his second semester. After spending a week at home doing nothing, it became clear that the lecturers were not calling off the strike anytime soon. Shetan decided to travel to Ayetoro. By this time, he had become less dependent on Mr. Anako and instead sought financial assistance from Shina in Lagos, as well as whatever support he could get from visits to his parents in Ayetoro.

Upon arriving in Ayetoro, Shetan was delighted to discover that Sayo was also in town. They had not seen each other for several years, maintaining their connection only through written correspondence. Seeing this as a valuable opportunity to reconnect and catch up, he immediately headed to Sayo parents' home in CRIN. With unwavering resolve, he knocked on the door, which was opened by Sayo's younger sister. She greeted him warmly and called out to Sayo, letting her know that Shetan had come to see her. As he waited, Shetan heard Sayo's mother's voice from the living room and leaned in to greet her politely.

As Shetan and Sayo embraced each other and sat on the pavement outside her parent's house, the years apart seemed to melt away, replaced by the warmth of their reunion.

"Sayo, you look exceptionally beautiful," Shetan said, his appreciation clearly visible in his eyes as he observed her glowing presence. The afternoon sunshine gently illuminated her, creating a delicate and magical radiance on her flawless face. Her hair flowed in beautiful undulating patterns, surrounding her face like a halo, while a delicate scent of wildflowers drifted about her, enhancing her inherent charm.

Sayo blushed in admiration. "I appreciate your compliments, Shetan." It has been an excessively long period since our last encounter. How is everything going with you"?

Shetan couldn't resist smiling in response to her captivating appearance. "I have been in good health, thank you." Seeing you now, I must say I have missed a genuine beauty." He couldn't take his eyes off her captivating presence, fixated on her. Upon catching up, Shetan saw the elegance in Sayo's gestures, the genuine and kind manner in which she spoke, and the radiance in her eyes that mirrored her inherent warmth. He was intrigued by her physical appeal and her inner beauty—her compassion, intellect, and elegance.

"I've been managing," Shetan replied with a smile. "University life has been hectic, as you can imagine. But seeing you again makes it all worth it."

Sayo's smile widened. "I've missed our conversations. It's good to have you back in Ayetoro."

"Indeed, it feels good to be back," Shetan agreed. "But enough about me. How have you been? Tell me everything."

Sayo's eyes gleamed excitedly as she vividly recalled her experiences at the Polytechnic in Owo. Her voice brimmed with passion as she detailed her academic accomplishments and the new friends she had made over the past years. Her words painted vivid pictures of her journey, drawing Shetan deeper into her world.

While they were talking, Shetan could not resist admiring the way her luminous grin illuminated her face and the elegant gestures of her hands as she spoke. His eyes wandered, momentarily entranced by the gentle curve of Sayo's cleavage, where a hint of delicate lace adorned her attire, accentuating her graceful figure with a subtle allure. Though momentarily distracted, Shetan quickly redirected his attention back to Sayo's words, captivated by her radiant beauty and the passion and intelligence that shone through in her every expression.

Their conversation flowed effortlessly, a testament to the bond they shared despite the years apart. But amidst the laughter and shared memories, an unexpected revelation lingered in the air, waiting to be addressed.

As Sayo's voice softened with a touch of uncertainty, Shetan's heart skipped a momentary pulse. "I forgot to inform you, Shetan," she said, her utterances lingering in the atmosphere, laden with an unexpressed burden.

As he waited for her next words, he felt a growing sense of suspense, like a knot tightening in his gut. Upon their arrival, they descended with an overwhelming force that seemed to stifle the surrounding atmosphere.

"I've found someone to marry," Sayo revealed, her tone tinged with a mix of excitement and apprehension.

Shetan had a sensation of the earth moving under him while feeling a heavy weight in his chest as his heart sank. Although it was warm where they were sitting outside, he felt a sudden chill as he fully grasped the reality of the situation. The comments lingered conspicuously, creating a sombre atmosphere that overshadowed their discourse and dampened the warmth of their shared recollections. At that moment, despite the delight and mutual fondness, Shetan had a pang of sorrow, as if something valuable had eluded his grasp, leaving behind just the reverberation of what may have been.

Sayo elucidated her choice, her eyes tinged with a certain melancholy. "My father has always desired me to marry someone from Ikole Ekiti, our place of origin. I couldn't resist seizing this opportunity that presented itself. I am determined not to overlook it, particularly in light of my father's desires," she stressed, her voice infused with a sense of remorse.

"I'm happy for you, Sayo," Shetan said, masking his disappointment with a forced smile. "It sounds like you've found new love at the Polytechnic."

Sayo noticed the change in Shetan's demeanour, her smile faltering slightly. "Shetan, is something wrong? You seem... distant."

Shetan hesitated, unsure of how to articulate his feelings without dampening the mood of their reunion. "It's just... surprising news, Sayo. I never expected you to settle down so soon. I had envisioned that we would patiently await the completion of our studies and subsequently construct our lives in unison," he said, his disillusionment palpable.

Sayo's expression softened, her eyes reflecting a mix of understanding and regret. "I know, Shetan. It wasn't an easy decision for me either. But sometimes, life takes unexpected turns."

Their conversation took on a more sombre tone as they navigated the delicate topic, both grappling with unspoken emotions beneath the surface. Despite their efforts to maintain the semblance of normalcy, the spectre of Sayo's impending marriage hung heavy in the air, casting a shadow over their reunion.

As they parted ways that evening, Shetan couldn't shake the disappointment lingering in his heart, silently mourning the loss of what could have been. And though their bond remained strong, tempered by years of friendship and shared memories, the revelation had irrevocably reshaped the trajectory of their relationship, casting doubt on the future that once seemed so certain.

After being in Ayetoro for two months, Shetan heard on the radio that lecturers had called off the strike, and students were expected at school the following week. Shetan, aware his father wouldn't be able to provide enough money for the remaining semester, borrowed a bicycle from Baba Idanre a day to Owena market so that he could go to the Tangyia farm, the new place where the government allocated lands to people to farm after *Ago Store*, so that he could bring some matured plantains from the farm for sale in the market for extra cash. It was time for him to use some of the principles he learned in his business class.

Pushing eight bunches of plantains along the Akure-Ondo express road, he would tinkle the bicycle bell whenever he spotted a car passing to draw their attention. He was about seven minutes from turning off the express to the road that leads to Ayetoro, just a few meters after Ipinlerere, when a white Benz 180 car parked in front of him.

"How much for these bunches of plantain?" The man in a white agbada asked Shetan as he stepped out of the owner's side.

"Which one, sir?" Shetan inquired.

"The whole thing", the man replied, his eyes never leaving the bunches, but occasionally, he stole glances at Shetan, obviously impressed with his comportment.

Shetan's sharp eyes did not miss the man's scrutinising gaze. However, he pretended not to notice but continued with the business in hand.

"Would you mind helping me load them into my car trunk?", the man asked politely after they had agreed on the price.

"With all pleasure, sir," Shetan replied, offering a courteous nod as he placed the items into the car's boot. As he did so, the man brought out his wallet, paid him the agreed price, and returned to his car when the last bunch was put in.

Shetan watched as the man entered his car and drove off; he promised himself there and then that he would persevere and work harder to complete his university education so that he, too, could buy a car one day. He hopped on the bicycle and cycled straight home. He cleaned up the bike and returned it to Baba Idanre, who lived opposite their house. He was happy he would not have to stress his mother about carrying the plantains to the market the next day.

Few people knew that Shetan was attending university, even though he was one of the first pupils from Ayetoro to achieve this milestone. However, he never let it go to his head. Unlike some boys from the polytechnic and colleges of education who often showed off by strolling around the village with their hands in their pockets, Shetan avoided such behavior. Instead, whenever he returned from the farm, he would head straight to relax at a friend's house located just after the Ayetoro bridge.

Some of the boys even doubted him, as he still went to the farm and brought home produce on his shoulder, something most boys his age in the village felt they were too big to do.

One thing Shetan always enjoyed whenever he was going back to school was how his mother used to fry twelve *mudus* of garri for him and prepare soup ingredients such as dry okro, egusi, and dried pepper, with a 4 litre of palm oil, among other things. Shetan also devoted some time to hunting so that he could take the roasted spoils with him.

Shetan had to move out of the store-turned-room in Agbooba, where he had lived with Bafe and Okonkwo for three semesters. He noticed that ever since they discovered he brought foodstuff whenever he returned from visiting his parents, they started locking away their own supplies in their bags. They would secretly cook and eat after depleting his provisions. At first, Shetan dismissed it as insignificant, but he eventually realized they were taking him for granted. Deciding he'd had enough, he moved out to live alone. This change allowed him to manage his food and the meagre resources at his disposal far more effectively.

Before his departure, Shetan made a heartfelt visit to Sayo to bid her goodbye. Deep inside, he carried a lingering doubt—a feeling that this might be their final meeting before she got married. Overwhelmed with sadness, he sought solace in their brief conversation, cherishing every moment they shared. As they parted ways, Shetan couldn't shake off the swirl of emotions—sadness, nostalgia, and a bittersweet sense of closure. It felt as though this farewell marked not just the end of a chapter but also the beginning of a new one.

At dawn on the day Shetan was set to return to university, he found himself surrounded by the warmth and love of his family. Mama Enitan, proud of her son's achievements and eager to support him, had prepared a variety of provisions and garri for his journey. His father also handed him some pocket money. Akanbi and Lanre, his younger brothers who were now in secondary school, accompanied him to the expressway, where he boarded a bus bound for Ondo. From there, he began the next leg of his journey to Oshogbo, where he finally boarded another bus to Ilorin.

Upon returning to the university, Shetan wholeheartedly immersed himself in his studies with a newfound sense of resolve. The university promptly arranged and conducted the examinations to provide sufficient time for the lecturers to mark the papers.

Shetan successfully overcame difficulties and uncertainties and performed well in his examinations by demonstrating concentration and hard work. As the institution hurried to gather and complete the collation of successful students, Shetan enthusiastically anticipated the next phase of his life, prepared to accept whatever the future had in store for him.

Chapter Fifteen: Life in Wukari

As soon as they finished their exams, some of the students started pressing for where they would serve, but for Shetan he left everything to fate as he had no one to influence his posting. As the day for call-up letters approached, a palpable tension settled over the campus, permeating the air with a sense of anticipation mixed with apprehension. The once vibrant Faculty of Business on the mini campus seemed to echo with the nervous murmurs of students, each one anxiously awaiting their fate. Among them, Shetan remained outwardly composed, but inwardly, a whirlwind of emotions churned within him. He had always left his destiny to fate, hoping against hope that he would not be posted too far from Ayetoro, the place he called home. Yet, as the day drew nearer, the uncertainty gnawed at him, casting a shadow over his usual calm demeanour.

The whole parking lot and every available space on the pavement of the students' affairs building was occupied by enthusiastic young graduates who had come for their call-up letters. All in groups of twos and threes engaged in animated discussions of previous experiences and what the future may bring. Some, however, were not as excited for the fear of being posted to the areas of Northern Nigeria where the recently introduced Sharia was a constant reason for unrest. Their faces wore a look of uncertainty.

For Shetan, who stood silently under one of the two nearby trees, nothing happening around him seemed to warrant his attention. Lost in thought, he leaned against the trunk with his palms resting behind him. However, his gaze eventually settled on the obituary poster of a student pasted on the yellow wall, and it stirred a flood of memories.

Bolanle's tragic fate struck a deep chord within him, serving as a sobering reminder of the grace he had often experienced on that very road. Countless times, he had travelled the same path without incident when visiting Mr Anako or his brother in Lagos. Yet, Bolanle's untimely death highlighted the unpredictable twists of fate awaiting students as they ventured beyond the boundaries of academia.

As he stood amidst the hushed whispers and solemn faces of his peers, Shetan could not help but feel a pang of sorrow for the loss of a fellow student, a life cut short before its time. But even amidst the grief and uncertainty, he knew that life must go on. With a heavy heart and a solemn resolve, he faced the distribution of the call-up letters, grappling with his fears and anxieties about the future.

"I knew it!" The voice of a jubilant lady could be heard outside the office as she pressed the letter to her chest.

"Me too," Another voice rang out.

"Come, let's go and drink Malt! This calls for celebration." The two ladies' faces were flushed with excitement. They had been posted to their choice state, Lagos.

"Wow! The land of endless opportunities! "Kemi, please forgive me for doubting you." the second lady said apologetically.

"Never mind, it's like that sometimes. Just trust me; my father has strong connections with the higher-ups. He's a retired General, you know." She said, adjusting her bag after putting the letter inside.

"Oh! Kemi, what would I have done without you? Thank you once again for your benevolence." she hugged her affectionately in appreciation.

"It's OK, Funmi. Let's leave now; we can't keep the driver waiting any longer." Both of them walked triumphantly away, absorbed in their own world.

When Shetan finally received his call up letter and saw that he was posted to Taraba State, he could not help but feel a bittersweet mixture of disappointment and determination. He retreated to the side of the building, where there were many Ashoka trees, referred to by many as Masquerade trees, to clear his mind a little before leaving.

"Shetan, where were you posted?" He heard a familiar voice and wondered who it might be

"Is that you, Shade?" He said, clearing his throat as he looked up and saw her. She wore a flowered button-down, thick long skirt with a tinge of red and a marching red blouse with puffy sleeves. She had no makeup on her face yet; her black, dense eyelashes and eyebrows were quite prominent.

"You haven't answered my question yet." She pursued further in her usual manner. Shetan had known her for that throughout their time as course-mates.

"Taraba, Taraba state." He said, rubbing his hands together anxiously.

"It's not too bad. You may find a home away from home there; you never can tell." She encouraged him.

"How about you?" Shetan asked.

"Zamfara…"

"Zamfara?" Shetan repeated, looking into her pale face.

"Yes, you heard me well. And I'll be leaving as soon as possible." She said indifferently.

"And the Sharia?" Shetan asked incredulously.

"I have no qualms with that. One can only drown in the river one goes to." She scratched her head, where she felt itchy and continued, "Besides, the law against theft cannot catch one who is not a thief. In fact, that law is not made for such individuals at all."

"Then, why are you pale if you're not bothered?" Shetan queried, and the proud gold-plated buttons of her skirt caught his eyes. They shone brightly under the reflection of the sun.

"Am I really pale?" Shade smiled.

"Yes, you are."

"Well, you're right, it's the lack of sleep. I've been helping a friend of mine who gave birth to twin babies for the past three days. I left the other side to this place because every single sound was tugging at my nerves."

"What a coincidence; a similar reason brought me here." Shetan exclaimed, "But you've changed my worldview. I had planned to serve in either the southwest or southeast area, which I'm familiar with and believe offers better opportunities. However, fate had other plans for me." He brought out his handkerchief and wiped his face.

"You don't have to feel disappointed because you think things went contrary to your expectation; consider it an act of God for your own greatness. Now that you're in the north-central area, why not make the best out of it?"

"Shade, to be honest with you, I must confess that I'm seriously disappointed with this deviation from my expectations."

"Look, Shetan, you're a business student. Take it or leave it, you must explore unfamiliar territories to make progress. No one ever builds an empire by moving in circles that some mistakenly call a comfort zone," she said. "I'm about to leave, but before I go, take a look at these trees where we're standing. They didn't choose to be here; people placed them here. But they chose to survive and thrive. Now, people come to them."

With that, she picked up her bag and walked away without looking back, leaving Shetan in a daze. While they had kept a respectful distance during their conversation, it did little to shield his senses from the soft, sweet fragrance that lingered in the air, a reminder of her presence.

Shade's argument was compelling, silencing all his fears under the weight of her words. He found comfort in the thought that the service would last only twelve months. This realisation reignited his spirit, filling him with the strength to face the challenges ahead.

The excitement of the journey from Akure to Wukari had kept Shetan awake for most of the night, yet he still had to rise as early as 4 a.m. to prepare. Finding someone willing to take him on a bike from Ayetoro to Akure at that hour was challenging, so when Jude volunteered, Shetan was overjoyed.

He arrived at the park around 4:30 a.m. The Benin Garage in Akure was already buzzing with activity and alive with energy, thanks to Jude's assistance, who made it happen for him to be there in time.

"When you get inside the garage, be careful with those agbero guys oo they have so many tricks up their sleeves," Jude warned before leaving.

As Shetan approached the garage, the air became filled with the loudness of honking horns, bustling crowds, and shouts of touts vying for passengers' attention. The park was a sprawling sand expanse, lined with rows of brightly coloured cars, buses and minibuses, each adorned with elaborate paintings and decorations.

"Oga, where you dey go?" One of the agberos asked as he quickly helped him with his bag.

"Where can I get a bus going to Wukari?" Shetan asked, following the man closely.

"Ha! Oga, car go better ooo as Wukari far well well." The man replied as he took Shetan to a dark blue 504 that was already loading people to Wukari.

The Peugeot 504 wagon car left Benin Garage at about 7:30 am, and Shetan initiated a conversation with the driver to ease the tension in his heart.

"Excuse me, oga driver, how long will it take to get to Wukari?"

"Well, at least twelve hours."

"Twelve hours? That's the longest journey I've ever taken!" He exclaimed, observing the green scenery that stretched out before him.

"Yes, it's quite a distance, particularly for a first-timer like you."

Shetan was baffled by the sight of the strange lump of fetish items tied beside the accelerator. He was fully convinced that this must be associated with the mysterious survivor without scratches by drivers in fatal accidents. He was tempted to ask the man but shelved the idea.

As the driver joined the main road and headed towards Owo, one of the passengers sitting behind Shetan shouted, *"Praise the Lord!"*

"Alleluia!" Everyone in the car chorused as she led them in prayers, committing the journey to God's hands.

As Shetan leaned back after the prayer on the well-worn co-pilot seat of the Peugeot 504 wagon, he was overcome by a feeling of unease. The next voyage seemed formidable, with extensive stretches of uncharted highways before him. As they left Akure, Shetan pondered what awaited them on the meandering route to Wukari. During the voyage, the Peugeot 504 wagon, rather than cruising, galloped over bumpy and uneven roads, experiencing vibrations and shocks that constantly reminded them of the challenging terrain they were crossing on the Akure-Owo route.

They travelled via Owo, where the streets were busy with activity, following the Odowara-Ishua Rd and Ipeme Ekpe-Ibillo-Isua-Oka towards Ogaminana-Abuja Rd/Okene-Auchi in Okene. With every round of the wheels, Shetan's apprehension intensified, his mind filled with ideas of uncertainty and the driver's excessive behaviour speed.

The inside of the automobile exuded a mix of anticipation and apprehension. The passengers engaged in lively conversation and laughter, their voices blending with the steady hum of the engine. Shetan became engaged in chats and was briefly diverted from his concerns by the companionship of his fellow passengers.

While travelling, they stopped at Okene due to the need for nourishment, where they took a break to eat and relax. The scent of piquant jollof rice and charred meat permeated the atmosphere, captivating Shetan's senses and briefly alleviating his unease.

Continuing their journey, they saw a lively hamlet by the side of the road, where ladies were selling delectable treats such as grilled plantains and akara from improvised kiosks. The alluring aroma of fried delicacies permeated the atmosphere, enticing Shetan to partake in a delicious snack throughout their voyage.

The scenery transformed as they proceeded on their trip, revealing undulating hills and expansive views. During their journey, they traversed tiny towns and villages, each providing a look into the multifaceted fabric of Nigerian culture.

Upon arriving in Makurdi around 4 pm, they came upon a gathering of musicians playing traditional drums on the roadside. The captivating beats of the drums enticed Shetan to participate in the festivities. He involuntarily tapped his feet to the rhythm as the music elevated his mood and alleviated some of his anxiety.

While travelling on the Enugu-Makurdi, the Peugeot 504 wagon had a terrifying moment when they narrowly avoided a collision with a reckless, luxurious bus driver. As they approached a tight curve, a fast-moving vehicle abruptly swerved into their lane, emitting a loud horn that pierced the air like an alarm. Instantly, the Peugeot driver made a sudden and quick manoeuvre to avoid a collision, causing the tyres to squeal against the tar as they dangerously slid towards the road's edge. Shetan's heart surged with fear as he prepared for the collision, seeing the world around him decelerating in the presence of imminent peril.

However, the two cars narrowly avoided a catastrophic collision by a tiny margin, which was a stroke of luck. As they abruptly stopped at the side of the road, Shetan felt relief, his heart pounding with adrenaline as he fully grasped the seriousness of the recent events. Following the near miss, the individuals in the Peugeot exchanged anxious looks, their expressions pallid with astonishment as they comprehended the seriousness of the circumstance. Temporarily, time seemed to stand still as they all took a minute to breathe, quietly expressing gratitude for narrowly avoiding a catastrophe.

As they continued their journey, the recollection of the almost-accident remained there, like a ghostly figure, serving as a clear reminder of how delicate life is and how uncertain the future may be on the road. Nevertheless, despite facing challenges, Shetan and his companions persisted in their journey with more remarkable tenacity. The close bond they developed due to the intense experience of almost facing a catastrophe strengthened their resolve.

At around 8:30 pm, they eventually reached Wukari, where Shetan was pleased to see that he was not the only one who had arrived at the Teacher Training College, which had been designated as the orientation camp. Shetan, feeling tired yet relieved, had a strong sense of achievement. Although he was initially hesitant, he successfully completed the lengthy and challenging journey, and as he entered the camp through the gate, he felt a fresh sense of strength and resolve.

He went straight to the registration point, where he was registered and given a kit containing a Khaki uniform, two pairs of white shorts and t-shirts, a pair of white canvas shoes and a jungle boot. His excitement mounted to the peak, and he muttered, *"So, I am now a Corper."*

The three weeks at the orientation camp felt like a military drill for Shetan. Every morning, the sound of the bugle would wake all the corps members early. Wearing the youth corps uniform each day brought him a sense of great pride. For once, he saw everyone dressed the same, regardless of their backgrounds or heritage. This uniformity gave him a sense of achievement, reminding him that they were all part of something bigger.

He remembered the day they went to bed hungry because his mother gave away the only one Naira they had left to eat that day. It was a rag day, a tradition where students dressed in tattered clothes and solicited donations. His mother, unfamiliar with the concept, took the student at face value when he explained that it was a day for university students to move around and raise funds for themselves. Without hesitation, she went into her room, retrieved the one Naira coin from under her pillow, and handed it over. Before doing so, she prayed earnestly to God, asking that one day, one of her sons would also have the privilege of being a university student who could participate in a rag day.

Shetan was furious at his mother's decision to give away their last coin, especially when they had planned to use it to settle part of their debt with Iya Lati and collect another mudu of garri on credit. Their previous debt for two mudus remained unpaid, and approaching Iya Lati that evening was out of the question. Unable to understand why his mother had acted contrary to their arrangement, Shetan was left to wrestle with his frustration and hunger. That night, they went to bed with empty stomachs, the weight of their predicament pressing down on them like an unbearable burden.

At the end of the three weeks of orientation, the new corps members were posted to various places of assignment and given a two-week break to go home and prepare for their new assignment. As part of the rules, corps members were expected to wear their uniform anytime they embarked on a journey. Even if they were not obliged to, Shetan saw it as a perfect time to make his family proud. Ayetoro respected and honoured youth corps members who had come over the years to serve in their village, and seeing one of their sons in corps uniform would be the talk of the village.

Shetan opted for a night bus to get home by the following afternoon. He was disappointed when he got to the park and was told the night bus was full.

"All the buses going from Wukari to Onitsha don full o, but if you go fit stand, no wahala, that one, na only half you go pay". One of the agberos stated.

When he heard this, he felt like turning back so that he could make the journey the following day. However, when he remembered that he was only paying half the price, he thought he might be lucky to get a seat if people alighted on the way. He lived to remember that journey as he stood all through the eight-hour journey from Wukari to Onitsha.

Shetan decided to alight at Owena market junction so that he could walk through the market to Ayetoro. He picked up his bag from the back of the bus that took him from Ondo; ensuring his cap was well positioned on his head, he adjusted his uniform. He knew that all eyes would be set on him at this moment and wanted to enjoy every bit of the admiration.

The market was virtually empty as he strolled through it. It was not a market day, and Shetan could not help but feel a sense of pride as he approached his mother's familiar stall. Pausing for a moment, a warm smile lit up his face as he looked at the point where part of his mother's sweat contributed to the full regalia he was wearing.

Unexpectedly, some onlookers expressed their surprise at the early arrival of Corps members in the village. However, as Shetan continued to traverse the village and crossed the Ayetoro bridge, a few individuals, upon recognising him, quickly closed the distance. A wave of excitement rippled through them, and soon, an enthusiastic chorus of "Corper! Corper!! Corper!!!" erupted, echoing just outside the C&S Church beside the water corporation.

One boy rushed to collect his bag as the commotion drew the attention of more villagers. Within seconds, a growing crowd gathered around Shetan, eager to catch a glimpse of the new Corps member. The news spread like wildfire, reaching the farthest corners of the village. Shetan became the centre of attention, and his presence became the hot topic of conversation among the villagers. The lively atmosphere in the village transformed into a celebration, with Shetan at its heart, making him the newfound hero and talk of the town.

Even Sayo's father, who had been against Shetan friendship with his second daughter, could not hide his admiration for him when he saw people gathered around Shetan as he walked through the village to his father's house. Everyone that met him on the way congratulated him as well. Some young boys and girls followed him to his house and were all full of joy that, at least, Ayetoro had been able to produce a "Corper".

Mama Enitan paused her kitchen chores as the sound of children's excitement outside grabbed her attention. She wondered what might be happening and decided to investigate.

As she walked to the front of the house, she caught sight of her son in his NYSC uniform, standing amidst the jubilant crowd with smiles. Tears of joy filled her eyes as she went down on her knees and worshipped the God of her ancestors and repeatedly said, Evesho, Ogboh ooo!

"Burotah' yan." Shetan prostrated and greeted his mother in their local language.

Mama Enitan gave her son a passionate hug and was full of

excitement. People watched in excitement as Shetan removed his NYSC cap and placed it on his mother's head! It was a moment that truly inspired the children, who clapped and clapped for mother and son.

Shetan gave money to Lanre to buy three packets of cabin biscuits and Nico sweet. Each of the children was given three cabin biscuits and two sweets as they went back to their various homes.

Still in full "Corper" regalia, Shetan went to greet Mrs. Okoro. She was so happy to see Shetan, and both of them shed tears of joy. Shetan knew within his heart that part of Mrs Okoro's tears was because of Evans, her son, whose whereabouts were still unknown.

 As Shetan left Mrs Okoro's house, he saw Mrs Chinedu looking fixedly at him with her mouth open, obviously shocked that *'that rag woman* could raise a child who has now become a Youth Corps member.

Before Shetan returned from Mrs. Okoro's house, Mama Enitan grabbed one of her chickens and slaughtered it to prepare a special dish for him. The two weeks Shetan spent in Ayetoro were quite memorable for him. Despite being a Corper, he still went to help his father on the farm, and many of the youths in the village came to him for motivation and advice.

Shetan was posted to GSS Wukari to teach the senior classes in Economics and Commerce. He will never forget his first-day experience in a hurry. When he got to the SS2 class, all the students in white and blue uniforms stood up to greet him. The gesture, though respectful, made him uncomfortable; many of them were older than him by several years. He could not hide his feelings.

Trying to mask his discomfort, Shetan greeted them with a strained smile.

"Good morning, everyone", He began, motioning for them to sit down. My name is Shetan Agbaje, and I am your new Economics and Commerce teacher. He introduced himself.

"Let me correct you, people, on one thing" He continued. "You needn't stand to greet me whenever I enter the class. Just remain seated and greet me from there."

His stay in Wukari was fun as the people of Wukari were warm and receptive. Shetan was so happy when he met two families from Ososo. After their weekly event, he went to the only studio then in Wukari to take pictures with two other corpers. As they entered the studio, a young boy alerted the owner about the presence of some customers in the Ososo language. After taking their pictures and settling the bill, Shetan introduced himself to the man, who was delighted to meet him. That was how Ogah Photos and Joseph welcomed him warmly and treated him like a brother. They regularly checked on him and ensured he felt comfortable and at home.

Chapter Sixteen: The Quest

After completing his 12 months of compulsory service in Wukari, Taraba State, Shetan decided to return to Ayetoro. He intended to take some time to rest before contemplating his next steps.

With the introduction of GSM mobile phones, communication became more accessible to people, although initially, they had to navigate hilly terrain to find reliable signals. For Shetan, this was no obstacle; he quickly identified a prime signal spot in Ikoshe where his Nokia 3310 could effortlessly connect for calls, making communication a breeze. To ensure its safety, he took his mobile phone to the farm daily, wrapping it in a nylon bag to protect it from the rain.

After a month in Ayetoro, Shetan felt it was time for him to search for greener pastures. Although the principal of GSS Wukari offered him a teaching job, he immediately declined the offer, feeling that it would take him too far from home. The ongoing conflict between the Jukum and Tiv people also heightened his fears for his safety.

Shetan called his elder brother Shina to inform him that he had completed his youth service and was considering coming to Lagos to explore opportunities. Shina was overjoyed to hear the news, celebrating the fact that they now had a graduate in the family.

Shetan moved to Lagos for greener pastures. He had been

coming to spend some days with his brother, mostly when he needed financial support while at university. Life in Lagos differed from that in Ibadan or Ilorin, where people went about their activities in an orderly manner.

Shetan felt the need to secure a white-collar job to support his parents, especially his mother, who had sacrificed so much for him. However, despite his persistent efforts, he only struggled to advance beyond the final stages of job interviews. He reached the final round twice with Logbon's bank but could not convince the managing director that he could bring substantial deposits to the bank. Undeterred, he persevered in his quest for a suitable job.

Shina, who was married to Oyimeh, also from Ososo, had three children when Shetan relocated to Lagos. Since Odun, Shetan's immediate sister was not yet married at that time, he decided to stay more with her in her one-room face-me-I-face-you accommodation. Shetan felt that Shina's room and parlour in Yakoyo were already congested. He arranged to stay with Odun from Monday to Friday and then visit Shina's place for the weekend.

Three years after relocating to Lagos, Shetan struggled in his job search. One particularly disheartening experience was an interview with CAPL, a subsidiary of UAC Foods, which was hiring management trainees. Amidst a large pool of applicants, Shetan passed the aptitude test and advanced to the final interview stage. During the one-to-one interview, he performed exceptionally well and was appointed as a group leader when the remaining twenty-six candidates were divided into two groups. Viewing this as an opportunity to demonstrate the skills and experience he had gained from years of interviews, Shetan impressed both the interviewers and his fellow group members. However, upon visiting their office to learn the interview outcome, he was shocked to discover that eight of the thirteen selected candidates were from his group, and his name was conspicuously missing from the list.

Recounting his disappointing experience with his sister at her World of Faith Christian bookshop in Onipanu, Shetan felt uneasy as he noticed a woman browsing the bookshelves. She intermittently glanced in his direction, making him wonder if she was eavesdropping on their conversation. Despite speaking in their local language, he couldn't shake off the feeling of being watched and found himself stealing glances at the woman, quickly averting his gaze whenever their eyes met.

Shetan would not have noticed that the woman was still around until she came to the counter to pay for the two books she had picked up. He was surprised that his sister knew the woman.

"Mummy Favour," as his sister called the woman, "this is my brother…my younger brother I told you about who is in Lagos for greener pasture after his youth service."

Odun finds it challenging to introduce Shetan as her younger brother. Despite being older by almost two and a half years, Shetan's towering height and robust build often overshadow this fact. Whenever she introduces him as her immediate younger brother, she can't help but glance at Shetan's face, anticipating his reaction. Yet, Shetan never fails to address her as "Aunty," maintaining a respectful demeanour regardless of his height and age difference.

"How are you, my son?" the woman inquired, her eyes scanning Shetan once more.

Shetan was taken aback when the *strange* woman divulged details about his private life. He couldn't help but marvel at how someone he'd never met could be so informed about him. The woman chuckled as he shared his struggles with finding employment during his three years in Lagos.

"My son, you're wasting your time searching for a good job in this country. If you humble yourself, you'll be able to travel abroad before the end of September," she advised.

She stood up, she settled her bill for the books and strolled towards the bus stop catch a bus.

Shetan was startled and, at the same time, laughed at what the woman said. He escorted the woman to the Onipanu Bus Stop, where she boarded a bus heading towards Yaba/Oyingbo. He pondered over her statement, struggling to comprehend how a young man, reliant on the support of his sister and brother, lacking an international passport as of April and having never set foot in an airport or witnessed an aeroplane taking off or landing, could manage to travel abroad *"before the end of September; I mean in five months' time!"*

His only maternal uncle residing in London had been stranded in Nigeria for over four years. Despite Uncle Dawson's persistent attempts to return, he faced continuous setbacks, having been deported more than twice during connecting flights en route to London.

Meanwhile, Shetan's sister had recently moved from Ilupeju to Bariga, seeking better living conditions. However, the new place offered little relief, with people still queuing early in the morning for the bathroom and latrine. The pit toilet was often in a deplorable state, forcing Shetan to manoeuvre carefully to deposit his waste atop the already full latrine contents. He longed for the simpler days in Ayetoro when he could comfortably relieve himself in the bushes rather than contend with the unpleasantness of the latrine at their house.

Two days after the encounter with Mummy Favour, Shetan decided to call her.

"My son, how are you doing?" Mummy Favour asked Shetan.

"I am fine, ma," Shetan replied.

Mummy Favour asked Shetan to come over to her place the following day, and the conversation they had made Shetan mystified.

After placing Shetan on three days of fasting and prayer, the woman reiterated the message she had conveyed to him at the bookstore, advising him to stay on the right path.

Feeling disheartened by the lack of progress after the CAPL setback, Shetan turned to Mr. Akinlade for job assistance. Mr Akinlade, who resided on Ogunji Street in Ilupeju, had long observed Shetan's commendable focus and determination. Impressed by Shetan's conduct, he couldn't resist asking why Shetan stood apart from other young men in the area who frequented internet cafes and engaged in fraudulent Yahoo Yahoo activities. His admiration grew upon learning that Shetan was a university graduate.

Mr Akinlade had just opened a printing press in Bariga. He was considering hiring a cashier to oversee the printing press as his print operator had been diverting some of the money. He agreed to employ Shetan at five thousand Naira a month. Initially, Shetan didn't want to take up the offer as the money was not up to what his colleagues who worked in the banking industry earned a day, but when he realised that he would be home doing nothing, he decided to take up the offer.

He started the work on the 10th of May, almost a month after the CAPL incident. He had a terrible dream the night before his first day at work and was shocked to meet the same face he saw in the dream chasing him with a cutlass at Mr Akinlade's printing press. He needed not to be told that he had to be careful as he perceived the man was diabolical. Shetan was able to reduce the leakages as he was in charge of all the financial transactions in the printing press, thereby increasing Mr Akinlade's profit.

Something happened in August that made Mr Akinlade relieve Shetan of his work. The first weekend of August, Shetan had gone to the burial of Mr Anako's mother in Ososo the first weekend of August. Due to the stress and the long journey back to Lagos on Sunday night, Shetan was tired the following morning and had a headache. He called Mr Akinlade on the phone, and after a few beeps, the phone connected.

"Who is on the line?" His raspy voice pierced through the earpiece, feigning ignorance of who the caller was.

"Good morning, sir, it's Shetan, sir."

"Ok! Ok! Ok! How are you? I hope there's no problem?"

"No, sir, it's just that I'm not feeling very well; I want your permission, sir. If you don't mind, sir, I won't be able to make it to work today."

"No problem, you can resume tomorrow." He said and disconnected the call.

Shetan never knew what was waiting for him the following day.

As soon as he resumed work, Mr Akinlade summoned Shetan to his main office.

"I want to thank you for what you have done for me since you started working with me about three months ago. I must confess that you have helped me put things in proper shape and saved me a lot of money in the process." He stated.

Shetan was wondering what could have led to such a speech. He was still thinking about this in his mind when the man continued.

However, given the current situation, the organisation no longer requires your services. I want to use this opportunity to thank you once again for all the good work you have done for us," he concluded.

Shetan was shocked! He least expected that he would be asked to leave without notice.

"Could it be because he decided to go for his uncle's mother burial and not return yesterday that warranted the sack"? He asked himself.

He thanked the man and left his office to collect his book in the printing section.

"Would you like me to intervene?" The man's wife asked Shetan with concern.

"Not to worry, ma'am. I know he has already made up his mind, and there's nothing we can do about it," Shetan said humbly.

Chapter Seventeen: The Gamble

Shetan went back home confused. Not knowing what to do next, he decided to count all the money he had in the case box. He had been saving it over the past three months while working for Mr Akinlade. Since he was not the one paying for house rent or food, he decided from the very first day he started working to save all his money with the little one he brought from Ayetoro. He was surprised to see that he had amassed the sum of thirty-seven thousand five hundred and forty Naira. Still contemplating what to do with the money, he decided not to tell his sister about being sacked by Mr Akinlade. He counted the money again and again as if doing that would increase the Naira notes. He placed the money back in the case and positioned it on the bookshelf on the wall.

While living with his sister in Ilupeju, Shetan would often browse the internet at a café whenever he had the funds to do so, considering that the internet was relatively new in the country at that time. In January of that year, having completed his internet session, he decided to spend the remaining few hours of the night browsing universities in England. With no specific purpose for his online time, he spontaneously applied to schools in England for a Master's degree despite lacking the funds for fees and expenses. Although he had received admission to the University of Lagos for MSc management earlier, he could not proceed due to the inability to raise the two hundred thousand Naira school fees.

A few days later, a university in London, England, requested his WAEC and undergraduate certificates. He went to the internet café the following week, and to his surprise, he discovered that he had been granted admission for a Graduate Certificate in Business. A pack arrived from the school at the Ogunji Street address two weeks later, containing the admission letter. However, after calculating the tuition fees, he realised they were more than twenty times higher than the local fees he could not raise just a few weeks back. Without hesitation, he laughed at his 'stupidity', tucked the admission letter among his books, and did not bother to look at it again.

As he was still contemplating what to do with the money through the night, a peculiar thought crossed his mind: *"Why not use the money to apply for an international passport and process a student visa since you already have an admission?"* He opened his eyes and scanned every nook and cranny of the room, half-expecting someone to be there offering such a piece of seemingly absurd advice.

However, the question lingered: *How on earth would he be able to raise the money for the flight, fees, and other expenditures?*

As soon as his sister left the house the following day, which was Wednesday, Shetan decided to look for the admission letter. It did not take him much time to locate it among his books. Reading through it, he smiled and told himself once again how foolish he was to think he would be able to raise such a huge amount of money. So many thoughts ran through his mind, and he did not know when he spoke out loudly that *"If I use the thirty-seven thousand, five hundred and forty Naira to apply for a student visa without telling anyone about it, at least if I am denied a visa, no one will know about it?"* He concluded.

He called Mr Akinlade the following day and thanked him for the little time he spent working with him. Like someone teleguided by invisible hands, Shetan went to the neighbouring state Immigration Centre in Ogun State, where he succeeded in getting an international passport on the same day. As soon as he got home, he called Anayo and told him his plans. He was happy to hear from Anayo that he had just gotten his admission letter to study in the UK.

Anayo helped put Shetan through the process, and within three days, Shetan gathered all the documents he could as supporting evidence. However, he needed to back up his application with a sponsor, and this gave him sleepless nights. He knew none of his siblings would be able to meet the criteria of a sponsor; even if they did, he did not want anyone of them to know about his plans. By Sunday night, just five days after being sacked, he resolved to seek help from Mr Akinlade. *"But how will a man who sacked him in less than a week give him a bank statement to back up his application?"* He pondered.

Shetan was the first to reach Mr. Akinlade's office early Monday morning. When Mr Akinlade saw him, he thought Shetan had come to plead for reinstatement. However, when Shetan explained his mission, Mr. Akinlade firmly stated that he could not release his bank account statement to him. However, a change of heart occurred when his wife intervened and, this time around, pleaded on Shetan's behalf. Eventually, Mr Akinlade reluctantly drove Shetan to the First Bank branch in Idumota and spoke to the bank manager, who printed out the company's account statement. Despite his initial reluctance, Mr. Akinlade handed it over to Shetan. "Make sure you handle it with care and don't allow it to fall into the hands of fraudsters," He sternly warned Shetan.

Grateful for the assistance, Shetan thanked the man and proceeded to the bus stop to catch a *molue* to Onipanu. Although he initially felt disheartened upon realising that the account was overdrawn when he examined the statement at home, he persuaded himself that including it would still be worth the risk.

The next day, precisely one week after being dismissed from his job, Shetan went to submit his visa application at the UK Visa Application Centre in Ikeja. He paid a fee of twenty thousand Naira for the application process. During this time, the UK operated a non-appearance policy for visa applications, requiring only the submission of documents. Applicants would then return a week later to receive the outcome.

As Shetan made his way back to Onipanu from the Centre in Ikeja, his mind buzzed with various scenarios. He acknowledged that, regardless of the outcome, he had followed his heart and was prepared to face the consequences. It was the most significant gamble he had ever taken in his life, pouring all his savings into something he wasn't even sure of. When his sister questioned his early departure from home that Tuesday morning, he simply explained that he needed to pick up items for the printing press.

For Shetan, the one-week waiting time seemed like an interminable void, with each passing minute filled with increasing tension. Uncertainty struck him, prompting him to question the wisdom of his decision to take such a tremendous gamble. However, amongst his profound uneasiness, he discovered a glimmer of comfort, realising that he had refrained from sharing his ideas with anybody or seeking financial assistance for the application. He carried a lonely burden, intensifying the weight of uncertainty that pressed on his shoulders.

Exactly two weeks after he was fired, Shetan waited in line at the Visa Centre in Ikeja, feeling anxious and nervous. Although he was the most casually dressed individual at the gathering, he could not avoid the noticeable atmosphere of fear. Observing the first three individuals in front of him break down in tears upon obtaining their passports drastically diminished his aspirations.

The officer's swift and purposeful actions intensified Shetan's unease as he firmly removed the papers from the envelope. Every passing instant was filled with ambiguity, intensifying Shetan's fear. His pulse raced with despair as he anxiously observed the officer's face when he opened the parcel.

Each crease of paper resonated inside the room, instilling Shetan with a sense of exhilaration. He gazed fixedly at the officer's face, meticulously searching for subtle hints or momentary reactions that might provide insight into the contents of the envelope. The room was filled with a palpable sense of expectancy, creating a heavy hush that seemed to hold everyone's breath, even Shetan.

The officer's deliberate tactics heightened the tension as time elapsed, and Shetan's mind became consumed with several possibilities. Positive results provided comfort, but more negative scenarios increased anxiety. He felt unsure and anxious, and as the officer carefully examined the contents of the letter, he felt a knot in his throat.

Only the gentle rustling of paper broke the profound silence in the room. Shetan nervously glanced back and forth between the officer's hands and face, desperately looking for some indication or clue about what was about to happen. The officer maintained a neutral demeanour, intensifying the suspense of the emerging event.

As the officer revealed the information, the level of tension reached its maximum point. Shetan felt suspended in time as the room remained unnaturally quiet. Every second elongated as if the whole cosmos had halted to see the crucial juncture in Shetan's existence. The atmosphere was filled with tension, so intense that Shetan impatiently anticipated the unpredictable decision.

"Congratulations, young man, you have been given a visa to the UK," the man declared.

His disbelief turned to astonishment when the officer handed him his documents. It felt like a dream to him. Shetan collected the envelope, and as soon as he got outside the gate, he called Shina, his older brother, to break the news. His brother was surprised.

"When did you apply?" his brother asked. "You were with me throughout the weekend and only left yesterday morning, but you didn't mention anything about applying for a visa?"

Mr Akinlade did not believe that the young man he had dismissed would, within fourteen days, be on his way to the UK. He did not conceal his disbelief when Shetan called him on the phone to share the news that he had been granted a visa to travel abroad.

"I want you to stop by my office so that I can see it," he stated.

Shetan took the passport to show Mr Akinlade and once again prostrated to thank him for his support. As soon as he arrived home, Shetan called Mummy Favour to share the good news. The woman was overjoyed for him and playfully teased him for doubting her words a few months ago. Shetan sincerely apologised to her and explained that it had been challenging for him to believe such prophecies.

Chapter Eighteen: The Trip Abroad

Surprisingly, Shetan managed to gather the N87,000 for the one-way KLM flight to London via Amsterdam and the required £250 Basic Travelling Allowance (BTA). He decided not to inform his mother about his trip abroad as he wanted to settle down before sharing the news, even though he had been visiting Ayetoro to check on his parents every Christmas.

The flight was scheduled to take off at 10 pm on the 29th of September, and Shina was already in Bariga to pick up Shetan at 5 pm so that he could have adequate time to settle at the airport before the take-off.

Oluchi, Evans' younger sister, stayed with Shetan and his sister while she prepared for her GCE exams in Lagos. In an unexpected twist, Shetan chose to keep his visa news a secret from Oluchi despite their close bond. Initially, Shetan's sister harboured suspicions about his relationship with Oluchi. Despite Shetan's efforts to assure her that their connection was purely platonic, his sister remained doubtful. This scepticism wasn't new; she had expelled Sayo from their Ayetoro home in the past, warning her against returning. This incident sparked controversy, leading Shetan to plead with their mother to caution her daughter, emphasizing that he had never interfered with her romantic relationships.

Given the circumstances, Shetan's sister was still accommodating Oluchi, being mindful of not disturbing Shetan, who she understood was only staying with her because of his difficulties in finding a job. Oluchi was filled with excitement as she prepared to stay with Shetan and his sister during her exams. Despite having a brother in Lagos who could have provided her with a place to stay, Shetan took the initiative to register her for the exams, and she deeply appreciated his support.

"I've noticed that your sister is always cold towards me; it's as if she isn't happy with me being here," remarked Oluchi.

"Oh, come on. Why must you think that way? Remember, she knows you and your parents in Ayetoro very well," Shetan replied.

Seizing the moment of their conversation, Shetan decided to disclose his upcoming travel plans to Oluchi.

"What if I tell you I'll be travelling to Kano next week?" he asked jokingly.

"For what?" Oluchi inquired in a tearful tone.

"I've just secured a job there, and I'll be starting next week on Wednesday," Shetan emphasized. Not allowing Oluchi to respond, he revealed that he would actually be travelling to the UK.

"Iro ni o, ehhhh!" she replied in Yoruba.

On the Friday preceding Shetan's journey to England, Oluchi accompanied him to Yaba market, where he purchased four shirts and three pairs of jeans. While navigating the bustling market, Shetan spotted a used leather bag he bought to store his belongings.

Shina decided to go through Oshodi to beat the traffic in Ikeja. Since Shetan had only one bag, it fit well in the boot of the BMW 318. Shetan left his phone for Oluchi since she did not have one. He was surprised to learn she was in tears when he later called her to inform her that he was at the airport.

"Why are you crying?" Shetan asked innocently.

"Nothing," she responded.

It was not until a few years later that Shetan came to know what made Oluchi sob like a baby the day he left for the UK.

The journey to the UK was easier than Shetan had ever envisaged. Even though he had never seen an aeroplane up close, except for the day he went with Shina to Briscoe when they passed through Mafoluku, Shetan was amazed at the size of the Boeing 727 that was left to rot away on one of the tarmacs. He wondered how such a colossal object could lift and fly. Shetan joined the queue to get cleared.

"What do you have in your bag?" the officer asked.

"Just clothes," he replied.

Shetan only went to the airport with one bag containing four shirts, two pairs of jeans, two shoes, and his documents. When he joined the line to check in his luggage, he was initially uneasy, but he strictly adhered to Uncle Dawson's advice to observe and mimic others.

When the flight attendant announced that the KLM flight was about to take off, fear overcame him, but he dared not show it so that people around him would not see him as a bush boy. As the Boeing taxied for take-off, Shetan closed his eyes and held his breath.

"Ladies and gentlemen, this is your captain speaking. We hope you enjoyed your time with us today. As we approach Heathrow Airport, please return to your seats and check your seatbelts are properly secured. Please store your tray tables, upright your seatbelt, and safely store all personal goods in the overhead bins or beneath the seat in front of you." The weather at Heathrow is clear, with a temperature of 18 degrees Celsius. We expect a smooth landing, but we understand that weather conditions might change, so we ask for your cooperation in following the crew's instructions.

Cabin crew: please prepare the cabin for landing.

Thank you for choosing to travel with us today. We appreciate your interest and wish you a pleasant stay in London or safe continued travels. "Welcome to Heathrow Airport." The captain concluded.

That was when it dawned on Shetan that he was half an hour away from his final destination.

When the flight touched down at Terminal 3, Shetan smoothly navigated through security and swiftly cleared by presenting his passport and admission documentation to the immigration officer. Following Uncle Dawson's advice, he hailed a black cab to transport him to the Great is the Lord Ministry in Stratford, where his uncle's acquaintance awaited his arrival. Travelling in a black cab driven by a white man proved an unexpected experience for Shetan, given the elevated status white individuals commanded in his homeland.

He vividly recalled how he and other children would eagerly line up to greet any white man they spotted in Ayetoro, particularly during road construction or water corporation repairs. Gathered together, they would wave and shout "oyibo, oyibo." Memories came flooding back of scrambling to catch a glimpse of Reverend Father Valentine Hynes whenever he visited from Idanre to conduct Mass at St. John's Catholic Church in Ayetoro.

Shetan couldn't forget the occasions when, as a young boy, he and Evans would contrive falsehoods during confession just to hear Fr. Hynes speak Yoruba, a sight that never failed to amuse the children. Witnessing a white man fluently speak and read from the Mass Book in Yoruba left an indelible impression on them all. At about 12:45 pm, the driver parked in front of the church and helped Shetan get his bag from the boot. Shetan paid him and thanked the white driver as he drove off.

Shetan knocked on the entrance door, and an old man opened it. He introduced himself to the man who ushered him into the church building. The old man was aware that Mr Obembe was expecting a visitor from Nigeria. Mr Obembe picked Shetan up at about 5:30 pm and headed to his house in Dagenham. Shetan could not believe that he was still in London.

"So, this is London," he repeated to himself again and again as they drove through the streets. The journey from Stratford to Dagenham in the grey Honda Accord car was one that Shetan enjoyed so much. What baffled Shetan was that all the roads were well-lit, and there was no single pothole on the road. Also, he wondered if people lived in the buildings as he was expecting a rowdy lifestyle like Lagos.

While in the car, Mr Obembe engaged Shetan in conversation about his trip and inquired about the well-being of his friend, Uncle Dawson. The journey took them through Gale Street, then turned right onto Woodward Road before merging onto Canonsleigh Road, eventually arriving at their destination. Mr Obembe parked the car and led Shetan inside, showing him to the smallest room in his three-bedroom house, where he instructed him to leave his bag. He then ushered Shetan to the kitchen, where he prepared Eba and egunsi soup, a meal that Shetan thoroughly enjoyed. Famished from the journey and unaccustomed to the mashed potato served on the plane, the meal was a welcome treat for Shetan.

Shetan could not begin his studies when he arrived in the UK on the last day of September. Not only was he unprepared for classes, but he also lacked the finances to enrol. Mr Obembe almost convinced him to forgo schooling.

"You don't need to bother going to school. Just work, earn about five thousand pounds, and I can help you with an arranged marriage to become a citizen," suggested Mr. Obembe.

However, a nagging thought reminded him of his primary purpose in London: to study. Yet, faced with the challenge of lacking the means to register, Shetan pondered his options. He took action by emailing London Metropolitan University in North London, requesting to defer his admission to February. Holding onto hope, he believed he might secure a job and save enough money to begin his studies in February.

Shetan used the opportunity to defer his admission by five months to do some menial jobs; however, he was mostly in Mr Obembe's office as an assistant without pay. Once or twice a week, he worked with Mr Obembe's business partner as a security officer.

Although Shetan was not paying for house rent, he did all the work in Mr Obembe's house. This ranged from washing his shirts and cleaning the house and the office to running errands for him. Something Mife always teased him about.

Chapter Nineteen: Escapade in London

Shetan was so happy when he finally enrolled in February and made the first deposit of five hundred pounds out of the school fees of seven thousand and two hundred British Pounds. It was not easy for Shetan to save that money within five months as he could not get a regular job due to all the house and office errands he had to run for Mr Obembe.

Starting his Master's degree proved to be a daunting challenge for Shetan as he struggled with the financial strain it imposed. The small income he earned from the menial work with Mr. Willy became increasingly insufficient, with a portion of his meagre wages arbitrarily deducted under the guise of taxes and National Insurance. Confused and frustrated by these deductions, especially since he had not been allowed to apply for a National Insurance Number, Shetan sought clarification from Mr Obembe. However, his attempt to question the deductions backfired, as he was labelled an ingrate and promptly dismissed from both the job and ejected from the house.

"How dare you ask why we deduct from your money?" Mr Obembe asked angrily.

"But", Shetan tried to explain when Mr Obembe cut in.

"Go to my house now, pack all your things and leave my house immediately, you ungrateful element," He roared.

Moving out that night when Shetan's first semester exams was less than a week away was what Shetan lived to remember. He took the bus home that evening and contemplated where he should go while on the bus.

Oladapo, who had previously managed IT tasks for Mr Obembe, grew frustrated by the lack of compensation for his efforts and eventually stopped accompanying him to the office. Despite Oladapo jokingly referring to Shetan as Mr. Obembe's houseboy, Shetan didn't take offence. Having shouldered greater responsibilities while living with Mr. Anako, he was accustomed to such remarks and didn't let them bother him.

Shetan took his phone out of his pocket and called Oladapo to share his situation. To his surprise, Oladapo informed him that his Aunty would allow Shetan to live with them until he found a place for himself.

Mrs Mercy smiled as she opened the door for Shetan; although her house was not too far from Mr Obembe's, Shetan was sweating profusely even though it was spring. The agony of dragging his bag was burdensome for him.

That marked the onset of Shetan's stay with Mrs. Mercy. The following day, armed with his resume, Shetan traversed the offices scattered along Dagenham A13, diligently seeking employment. However, all he encountered were assurances of potential callbacks whenever vacancies arose. Nonetheless, after two months of persistence, fortune smiled upon him, securing a night shift position with a cab company situated on William Street in NW1. While the nocturnal schedule was unfamiliar territory, the prospect of earning income to cover his expenses filled him with immense joy.

Shetan was writing his second-semester examination when Dr Wande, who was like a father to all the black students in the university, called him to his office.

I see you as someone responsible and passionate about everything you do. I want to let you know that a new Master's course is starting this September, and I strongly encourage you to apply," Dr. Wande concluded.

Shetan stared at him in disbelief. How could a man aware of his struggles to meet the quarterly instalment payments suggest taking on another degree? There were times when Shetan couldn't afford the payments, leaving his ID card blocked and barring him from attending some lectures. The suggestion felt almost impossible to consider.

"I know what is going on in your mind, Shetan," Dr Wande said. "But come to think of it, the university is just introducing this course, and instead of doing six modules, you will do only four since you have covered two of the modules in your current study." He said.

"But sir," Shetan said, trying to explain to him that he was still struggling when Dr. Wande cut him short.

"But what?" Dr Wande interrupted him.

"Don't think of the tuition fees; think of the opportunities this will give you in the job market." He concluded.

That was how Shetan got two Master's degrees within twenty-five months of arriving in London.

After completing the two Master's degrees, Shetan continued working at his night customer service job. He could now work from home rather than travelling to Williams Street in NW1 from East London, reducing journey time and transport costs.

Chapter Twenty: Return to Nigeria

Three years after leaving Nigeria, and now that he had completed his studies working and paid off his school fees, Shetan felt the need to go home and greet his parents. Although he was constantly in touch with his mother and sent her a monthly stipend, he believed his physical presence would bring them immense joy and comfort. The longing to see familiar faces and reconnect with the roots of his upbringing grew stronger with each passing day. Shetan decided it was time to plan a visit back to Nigeria.

His journey back home held significance beyond just familial reunions. Shetan envisioned sharing his achievements and the challenges he met along the way. The desire to make his parents proud and express his gratitude for their unwavering support fueled his determination to embark on this journey.

As he prepared for his homecoming, Shetan reminisced about his childhood memories, the lessons imparted by his parents, and the sacrifices they made to provide him with an education. The anticipation of reuniting with his roots, the familiar sights and sounds, and the warmth of his family embraced him with a profound sense of nostalgia.

Shetan knew that this journey was not just about fulfilling a personal longing but a tribute to his parents' unwavering love and sacrifices. It was a celebration of the dreams they had nurtured and the aspirations he had pursued, now manifesting in his successful academic accomplishments.

With a heart filled with gratitude and excitement, Shetan emptied his bank account, bought some things for his family members, and boarded the flight to Nigeria.

He had not seen his mother for nearly a year before departing Lagos for London. Meanwhile, he maintained close communication with Oluchi, with whom he had formed a strong bond.

Shina picked him up and took him to his house in Ikorodu, Lagos. When Shetan got to Shina's place that evening, he handed over the sum of four thousand five hundred British Pounds he had made since he finished paying his school fees to him.

"I want to ensure our parents start their housing project in Ososo." Shetan told his elder brother.

"I have been nursing the same idea but lacking the power of execution; I kept my mouth shut all this while," Shina replied excitedly. "Now that light has come through you, you have my full support!"

The next day after arriving in Nigeria, Shetan went to visit Mummy Favour. He brought her a gift and some money as a gesture of gratitude. She was overjoyed to see him, offering heartfelt prayers for continued blessings in his life.

Little did Shetan know that this would be the last time he would see her. Seven months later, Mummy Favour passed away from complications related to a dental procedure, a tragic infection that took her life far too soon. Shetan would forever be grateful to her for the guidance and wisdom she had shared with him, especially her uncanny ability to foresee his path. Her loss was a sobering reminder of how fleeting life is, and how quickly moments with those who shape our lives can slip away.

On the third day, Shetan and Shina embarked on their journey back to Ayetoro. Mama Enitan's joy knew no bounds upon reuniting with her two sons, especially Shetan, whom she hadn't seen in four years—the same duration since she last saw Shina. Overwhelmed with gratitude, Mama Enitan decided to sacrifice one of her goats to thank the God of her ancestors for making her dream come true.

Meanwhile, Shetan's other two younger brothers are now in higher institutions. Akanbi had chosen to pursue a path towards priesthood, a profession cherished by Mr Agbaje, while the youngest had gained admission to Owo Poly in Owo. Both were elated to see their two elder brothers again, their happiness evident in their warm welcome.

Shetan stood before the dilapidated building, a relic of his past that had sheltered him for nearly two decades. Memories flooded back as he questioned whether this crumbling structure was the same haven that shaped his formative years. Shetan found himself transported back to a time when every day was a battle against adversity. The once-promising facade of the building now mirrored the stagnation that had gripped his birth place since he departed for Lagos following his Youth Service, setting out on a journey that took him far from these modest origins. Returning after just four years, Shetan was shocked by how little had changed. The overwhelming sensation of weakness in the air served as a vivid reminder of the difficulties he had faced in forging a new life in distant lands. Each crack in the worn walls spoke stories of strength and resolve, compelling him to reflect on the distance he had come, both geographically and metaphorically.

He went around to greet their neighbours, who were genuinely happy to see him.

When Mr Agbaje returned from the farm and saw the BMW 318 parked outside his house, he knew his first son was around.

"This young man should at least have informed me of his coming. I would have prepared some things for his comfort. Did my wife hear and forget to mention it?" he soliloquised. However, upon entering the house and spotting Shina and Shetan, his surprise quickly gave way to genuine happiness.

After dinner that evening, father and sons sat outside in his usual place of rest before going to bed. Many important decisions about the family had been made in the past, and this night was destined to be one of them.

"Ita," Shina said, going straight to the subject. Shetan and I have discussed it, and we think it's time you got us our own family house in Ososo."

Mr Agbaje cleared his throat, "Thank you, my sons, for raising the issue of building a house in Ososo. I have been planning this for years. However, I plan to build a house in Orugbe, where no one has moved to yet."

Shina and Shetan knew their father was not keen on this project, but the pressure they applied made him change his mind.

"But on one condition," he said, "I will take a bricklayer from Ayetoro to Ososo."

Shetan was overjoyed that evening when his father finally agreed to build a house in Ososo.

"Ita," Shina called their father with a smile on his face, "God has blessed you with sons who are ready and willing to support you on this project. Shetan brought some money for that purpose. All you need now is execution."

Eager to savour the moment, Shetan decided to visit the farm the next day. Uncertain when such an opportunity might come again, he was determined to make the most of it. As he headed to the farm with Shina, memories of his cherished catapult from his youthful days in Ayetoro flooded his mind. To his surprise, he discovered that his once-sharp catapulting skills had dulled over time. Yet, holding the catapult again brought him immense joy, rekindling the carefree spirit of his childhood.

Oluchi was already in the polytechnic when Shetan arrived in Nigeria. On their way back to Lagos, Shetan decided to make a stop in Ilesha and boarded a car to visit Oluchi. He informed Shina that he would meet him later in Lagos.

He stayed with Oluchi over the weekend, and both of them could not resist the bond they had developed over the years.

"I said I won't ask you this question until I return."

"What question?" Oluchi's curiosity mounted.

"Why were you crying the day I left Nigeria?"

"Oh, that?" she sighed, "I see my brother Evans in you. So, when you teased me with that Kano job, something churned in my stomach. When you finally left, I felt alone in the world." She said with misty eyes.

"It's alright. You don't have to feel lonely anymore; I'm here now." Shetan comforted, feeling deeply touched.

After Shetan left her place that Sunday morning, Oluchi decided to travel to Ayetoro to discuss the matter with her parents. Unfortunately, when Oluchi told her parents of Shetan's intention to marry her, they swiftly opposed and rejected her proposal.

"Can you repeat what you just told me"? Mrs Okoro asked her only daughter.

Looking at Oluchi heretically, she wondered if her daughter knew the cultural implication of what she was telling her.

"So, you mean you want to marry someone who is not even from the next village but a state far away from ours?" Mrs Okoro said.

I have nothing against him or his family," she said. "He's well brought up and comes from a good family. But the fact that we don't come from the same place or speak the same language makes marrying him impossible".

While Mrs Okoro took the time to explain the cultural implications to Oluchi, Mr Okoro did not even give both mother and daughter any audience when his wife raised it with him. He told them that it had never happened in his lineage that their daughters married from outside, and he would never be the first to start it.

That was how the dream of Shetan and Oluchi sealing the bond they shared became shattered, and Oluchi was made to marry a man from the same area.

Omoyemi was the daughter of Mrs. Enitan's very good friend who graduated from Obafemi Awolowo University. She was about five and a half feet tall with the polished air of a city dweller. In the instance of her mother, who had a previous discussion with Mrs. Enitan, she came to return the basket of soup items she had forgotten at home. That evening, she was connected to Shetan via a video call, and when he saw her, he could not conceal his excitement. Omoyemi looked everything like Sayo and a little of Oluchi. He was almost incoherent in their discussion. That was how they found instant love in each other. The following year, Shetan travelled back to Nigeria and got married.

Chapter Twenty-One: The light goes off

S hetan continued his work from home with the same company and had just woken up after his night shift when his wife told him a particular number had been trying to reach him.

"How can someone call five times without leaving a message?" he wondered, then decided to return the call.

"Agberan Broda oo", the receiver said.

"Agberan oo", Shetan replied, puzzled by the caller's use of their local language despite never speaking to her before.

"Iyan is sick and has been taken to the local clinic in Ososo." the lady said sorrowfully.

"Which Iyan" Shetan asked

"Your Mother, sir" The woman replied.

Shetan's hand trembled, nearly dropping the phone. The words hit him like a cold wave, and for a moment, everything around him seemed to blur. His mind raced, struggling to process the shocking news. "My mother is sick?" he thought, disbelief and worry washing over him in equal measure. His heart pounded in his chest, and he could barely make sense of the lady's sorrowful tone. The thought of his mother, usually so strong and healthy, being taken to the hospital was overwhelming. He struggled to steady his hand, fighting to regain control, but the weight of the news left him feeling numb and helpless.

"But I spoke with her barely twenty-four hours ago!" he exclaimed, shocked by the sudden news of her illness.

"Could you please hand the phone to my mother?" Shetan's voice wavered, his grip tightening on the phone as a wave of anxiety washed over him.

Mama Enitan had always been active and strong, effortlessly managing both farm work and household chores. She rarely fell ill, aside from the occasional headache or bout of malaria. Throughout Shetan's life, he had never seen his mother sick enough to need hospitalization. Her energy seemed endless, and he often marveled at her resilience. Shetan would sometimes wonder where she found the strength to keep going, amazed by her ability to overcome any obstacle.

The only time he could recall her visiting the hospital was when she contracted the same bacterial infection as Shina while nursing him. But even then, she recovered quickly, bouncing back the very next day after receiving an injection.

The lady passed the phone to Mama Enitan.

Shetan, I felt weak and tired, then suddenly dizzy, and the next thing I knew, I was in the hospital," Mama Enitan explained, her voice low and steady as she tried to make sense of what had happened.

"Don't worry, Iyan," Shetan reassured her. "You'll get the best care, and everything will be alright".

Shetan spoke with the doctor, who assured him it was mere fatigue and that he would do all he could to ensure she was well and could return home very soon. Shetan thanked the doctor and went back to sleep. However, later that afternoon, the same number called again to inform Shetan that his mother's situation had deteriorated. She had been transferred to a bigger hospital in Ibillo for further assessment.

Akanbi had just arrived in Ibadan to begin preparing for his missionary work when he received the distressing news that his mother had been admitted to the hospital. Without hesitation, he sought permission from his superior to visit her. Upon reaching the hospital, he was confronted with the news that his mother might need to be transferred to the Specialist Hospital in Irrua. With swift resolve, he arranged for a taxi and sat by Mama Enitan's side in the back seat, his mind racing with worry.

As they made their way to the hospital, Akanbi couldn't help but reflect on the recent memories of his mother's vibrant presence at his ordination in Ibadan and the thanksgiving ceremony in Ososo, which had taken place barely a month ago. He was struck by the sudden turn of events. Mama Enitan's status in the village had changed almost overnight after Akanbi was ordained as a Catholic priest, earning her the affectionate title of "Iyin Father" and winning her the admiration of the villagers in both Ososo and Ayetoro.

As the journey continued, Akanbi sat close to his mother, offering her words of comfort and assurance that she would be alright. Meanwhile, Ireti, who sat at the front with the driver, shared with Akanbi the harrowing account of how Mama Enitan had suddenly collapsed while feeding her fowls in front of their house. The abruptness of the incident added to Akanbi's concern, yet he remained resolute in his faith and vowed to support his mother through this challenging time. With each passing moment, his love and concern for her deepened, motivating him to ensure she received the best care possible.

"Doctor, please do all you can to make sure that she is okay. Don't worry about the bill, as everything will be settled," Akanbi told the doctor on duty.

"We will do all we can, Padre," the doctor on duty replied reverently as he wore his cassock.

He looked at his once vibrant and energetic mother again and shook his head. He knew something was amiss and could sense the thick, dark cloud around her. After the doctor had attended to her and she was placed on a drip, he sprinkled holy water on his mother and blessed her with a sign of the cross. He could see how peaceful his mother was when the water touched her.

"Please, take care of Iyan; I'll come back in a few days," he said to Ireti, his voice tinged with concern. "I have some urgent matters to attend to in Ibadan," he concluded.

He had to rush back to Ibadan to complete his paperwork before starting his missionary journey to the Central African Republic.

As he quietly turned to leave the ward, his mother called him back.

"Pray for me, my son, remember me in your prayers," Mama Enitan pleaded, her voice trembling, her eyes filled with concern. "Make sure you continuously pray for me, as I do not like what I see around me. It has always been my dream to see you all achieve your goals and become great in life. I thank God that Shetan came home to marry Omoyemi last year, and Shina is doing well in Lagos. Above all, my joy knew no bounds when you were ordained just a month ago. But with the dark cloud surrounding this place..." Mama

Enitan's voice faltered as she started coughing, unable to finish her statement when she started coughing.

The doctor was summoned, and Mama Enitan was advised to rest. Tearfully, she watched her third son, clad in his cassock, exit the ward. Despite her pain, Mama Enitan summoned a smile, her heart swelling with pride as she watched people come to Akanbi, asking him to lay hands on them and pray for their sick loved ones. The sight filled her with a deep sense of pride, knowing that her son was now a source of hope and healing for others.

"Even if his ordination was the last achievement I would witness in my children," she whispered softly, almost inaudibly, "I am more than satisfied."

After six days of his mother's hospitalisation, Shetan, who was thousands of miles away from home, grew increasingly concerned about her prolonged stay in the hospital. Unable to comprehend why she remained hospitalised for such an extended period, he reached a breaking point. Desperate for answers, he purchased a calling card and called Ireti, who had been with her right from the moment she collapsed.

Shetan was a bit relieved when he heard that Odun came from Lagos to stay with their mother, but she had gone to purchase the drugs the doctor prescribed. However, as Shetan spoke with his mother that evening, he was taken aback by the sound of her voice. It starkly contrasted the vibrant and energetic tone he was accustomed to hearing from her. Her voice now carried a weight of illness and fatigue, causing Shetan to worry even more. It seemed as though his mother had been battling sickness for far longer than just the six days she had been in the hospital. This sudden transformation in her voice only heightened Shetan's anxiety, leaving him grappling with concern for her well-being from afar.

"I will be okay, my son." Mama Enitan assured Shetan, her voice croaky but firm.

"Iyan, do you want me to come home and see you?" He asked.

"No, no, no, my son. Don't bother to come at all." She bluntly said with a shrug.

The following evening, the Friday of the second week of August, was one Shetan won't forget in a hurry. He was in the middle of finishing his lunch when his phone rang twice and was cut off. He needed not to be told it was a call from the lady looking after his mother in the hospital. He picked up his phone and called the lady. Shetan almost fainted when he heard that his mother had been placed on a life support machine.

"Broda, Iyan was struggling for breath just a few minutes ago, and the doctor has placed something over her head that has a pipe connected to one machine like that," She said, her voice choked with tears.

"Can you put me through to the doctor, please?" Shetan asked Ireti, with tears coming down his cheek.

Luckily, the doctor was still there, and Ireti passed the phone over to him.

"Hello, doctor," he said anxiously, his voice trembling. "I am one of Mama's children. Please, I implore you to do everything in your power to save her life. She means everything to me, and I cannot bear the thought of losing her now."

"I will try my best," the doctor assured him, his voice steady but firm. "But as a man, you must prepare your mind for any eventuality." The doctor concluded bluntly.

Restless and consumed by worry, Shetan reached out to Odun, who informed him that she had procured all the medications prescribed by the doctor. He also spoke with Akanbi, who briefed him on their mother's condition before leaving the hospital to start preparations for his missionary work.

"We should continue to pray for her" He concluded.

He called Shina to inform him of the latest event, and he was told that Lanre, their last born, was on his way to Irrua to join Odun and Ireti.

Shetan called Odun almost every half an hour, desperate for updates on his mother's condition. His heart pounded with every ring, each moment feeling like an eternity. During one of the calls, Odun mentioned that Mama Enitan, despite being connected to a life support machine, had stirred slightly, indicating she wanted to know who was calling. When Odun informed her that it was Shetan, a faint glimmer of recognition seemed to pass through her tired eyes.

Mama Enitan, still hooked to the life support machine, managed to signal her desire to speak with her son. With the nurse's help, the machine was momentarily paused, allowing Shetan's voice to reach her.

"Iyan, it's me," Shetan said softly, his voice filled with tenderness and concern.

Mama Enitan tried to respond, but her words were lost in a jumble of mumbled sounds. The effort was evident as she strained to communicate, a poignant moment that underscored the severity of her condition and the depth of her love for her son.

Shetan tried to see if Mama Enitan could say a word but failed. When the nurse in charge realised she was getting weak, she picked up the phone and told Shetan the woman needed to rest. Shetan could feel that something terrible was about to happen but did not want to think of losing the most precious person in his life at that point in time! Not even Omoyemi, his wife, who is eight-month-old pregnant, could soothe him to sleep as he rolled over and over again in his bed through the night.

"Why not try and sleep, my husband? You should know she is a mother to us all; she is going to be okay," She said as she tried to soothe him.

"How can I sleep with my mother in such a condition in the hospital?" he responded tearfully. "Tell me, where would such sleep come from?"

"You see, everyone dearly loves Mama," Omoyemi continued, her voice filled with reassurance. "I'll never forget the warmth she showed me when I first visited Ososo to meet her before our wedding. She embraced me like her own daughter and treated me with such kindness. I can still recall her vibrant presence during our traditional wedding in my hometown, radiating joy and vitality. It's hard to imagine that she was so full of life just thirteen months ago. But I want you to believe that she'll pull through," She concluded, striving to alleviate the tension in their bedroom.

He recalled all the sacrifices his mother had made for him and his siblings. He didn't remember when he had fallen asleep, but during his rest, Shetan experienced a disturbing nightmare. In the dream, he found himself standing powerless next to his mother's hospital bed, helplessly watching her vital signs rapidly decline despite the frantic efforts of the medical personnel. The harsh beeping of machines echoed in his ears, heightening the sense of impending doom, and a deep despair consumed his heart.

Suddenly, he was jolted awake by a shrill scream that pierced the darkness of his bedroom. Startled, he shot up in bed, his heart racing, drenched in sweat. For a moment, he couldn't process what had happened. Then, he realized with a shock that the sound disrupting the silence of the night had come from his own throat. Trembling, Shetan tried to shake off the lingering effects of the terrifying dream, his breath shallow and uneven as he struggled to regain composure, still gripped by the intense fear that refused to let go.

Glancing at the glowing digits on the bedside clock, Shetan noted with a heavy heart that it was only 3 a.m. The urge to contact Lanre, who had arrived at their mother's bedside the previous night, tugged at him, but he hesitated, deeming it too early to disturb him.

Shetan's abrupt awakening startled Omoyemi, who had been dozing fitfully beside him. She reached out to touch his trembling form; concern etched across her features.

"My crown, what happened? Why did you scream like that?" she asked, her voice thick with worry.

Shetan struggled to steady his ragged breaths; his eyes wide with lingering fear from the nightmare. "I-I had a terrible dream," he stammered, his voice shaky. "It was about Mama... she was... I thought... I thought I lost her."

Omoyemi's grip tightened on his hand, her own heart racing with empathy for her husband's distress.

"Oh, my dear," she whispered soothingly, pulling him close.

"It was just a dream. Mama is going to be okay, remember? We're all here for her, praying for her recovery."

Shetan nodded, trying to calm his heart pounding as he clung to his wife's comforting embrace.

"I know, I know," he murmured, his voice still trembling. "But it felt so real... I just couldn't shake it off. I saw my mother; it was so clear."

Omoyemi gently kissed his forehead, her love for him evident in the tender gesture. "Let's try to get some rest," she suggested softly.

With a nod, Shetan allowed himself to be drawn back into her arms, finding solace in her presence as they both sought refuge from the lingering shadows of the night.

At around 5:45 am on that fateful Sunday, Shetan's phone abruptly rang, jolting him from his sleep. As he frantically reached for his phone to see who had flashed him, the call from Shina came through. With trembling hands, he answered the call from his older brother, sensing the weight of the news about to be delivered.

"Shetan, it's me, Shina," came the sombre voice from the other end of the line.

Shetan's breath caught in his throat as he braced himself for the inevitable but could still summon courage. "Egbon, how are you"? His voice was barely above a whisper.

There was a heavy pause before Shina spoke again, his words laden with sorrow. "I'm sorry, brother. It's about Iyan... she's gone."

Shetan felt as though the ground had been pulled from beneath him, his heart wrenching with anguish at the confirmation of his worst fears. "No... no, it can't be true," he murmured, his voice cracking with emotion.

Shina's voice was gentle yet filled with grief as he offered words of solace. "Iyan passed away about ten minutes ago," he said as the call ended.

Tears flowed freely down Shetan's cheeks as he struggled to comprehend the enormity of the loss.

"Iyan ooo, iyan ooo!" He moaned, beating his chest.

"Why didn't you wait a little longer... Iyan oo! Does it mean you're gone... Just like that..." He choked and could not control his tears and did not know when he started crying like a baby!

"I... I can't believe she's gone," he whispered hoarsely as Omoyemi asked him what was wrong, his words barely audible amidst the waves of sorrow crashing over him.

"How could mere tiredness lead to the end of his mother?" Shetan pondered bitterly, his heart heavy with disbelief and anguish. Just thirteen months ago, she had been a vibrant presence at his traditional wedding, bustling about the market to buy all the items for the bride price and radiating joy and pride at Akanbi's church Thanksgiving service just a month ago. The memory of her active involvement in their family celebrations only served to deepen Shetan's sense of loss.

What pained him most was the fact that he had kept his wife's first pregnancy a secret from his mother, intending it to be a joyful surprise for her. Even when Mama Enitan jokingly inquired about two months ago when he would become a father, Shetan reassured her with a smile, promising that it would be "very, very soon." Little did he know that she would never live to hear the cries of her newborn grandchild, robbed of the opportunity to share in the joy of this new life. The weight of this missed opportunity weighed heavily on Shetan's heart, adding an extra layer of sorrow to his already overwhelming grief.

For days on end, Shetan grappled with the incomprehensible reality of his mother's death. Deep within his soul, he harboured a conviction that her death was not merely a result of ordinary circumstances. The shock and pain of losing Mama Enitan were profound, casting a shadow of sorrow over Shetan's days.

Adding to his anguish was the cruel twist of fate that prevented him from attending his mother's burial. With his wife eight months pregnant, Shetan found himself torn between the desire to mourn his mother's passing and the responsibility of caring for his growing family. The inability to bid his final farewell to his beloved mother in person weighed heavily on his heart, intensifying his sorrow and threatening to engulf him in a cloud of despair. The profound sense of loss, coupled with the constraints of his current situation, left Shetan teetering on the brink of depression, struggling to find solace amidst the overwhelming waves of grief.

The news quickly reached Ososo that Mama Enitan had died. Everyone was shocked to hear that a woman who was dancing in the church barely one month ago was no longer in their midst.

Mama Enitan was a generous woman, deeply loved by her community. Since moving permanently to Ososo three years ago, her home had become a gathering place for extended family members and friends, all eager to share meals and laughter in her company. Known for her warm hospitality, Mama Enitan made sure that no one ever left her house hungry, always offering food to her visitors. Her spirit of generosity was a defining part of her character, and it brought her immense joy to see her loved ones enjoying hearty meals and engaging in lively conversations under her roof.

She never lacked for anything, as Shetan always ensured she had more than enough food at home. With her home standing as a beacon of warmth and hospitality in the community, Mama Enitan's legacy of generosity continued to flourish, touching the lives of everyone who crossed her threshold.

Akanbi shared with his siblings his heartfelt desire to honour their mother by officiating her burial ceremony, expressing his wish to do so one week after her passing. He explained that as he had recently been transferred to a neighbouring African country for his missionary work, it would be challenging for him to make multiple trips back and forth. Thus, holding the funeral within a week would allow him to fulfil his duties as the officiating Priest without the logistical difficulties of travel.

The family unanimously embraced Akanbi's proposal, recognising the significance of his wish to officiate their mother's burial. Shetan, in particular, took it upon himself to ensure that every aspect of the funeral arrangements was meticulously attended to. Feeling a profound sense of indebtedness to his mother, he spared no effort in providing nearly all the resources needed to ensure her a dignified and befitting farewell.

As the day of the funeral dawned, Mama Enitan's remains were transported in an ambulance from Irrua Specialist Hospital to Ososo, with Lanre and some other boys on the bus. Bimpe could not hide her emotions as she cried profusely. Both young and old lined the Ajoyo-Okhe road, their grief palpable as they awaited the arrival of the ambulance. As the white Toyota Hiace ambulance approached Ososo, a collective wail of mourning pierced the air, mingling with solemn hymns, local drums and songs, and heartfelt farewell cries.

Akanbi stepped out of Shina's car, led the ambulance, and joined the multitude following it as it headed towards the market square in Okhe. He intermittently sprinkled Holy Water on them, followed by the sign of the cross. The procession continued through the village, traversing Ajoyo to Yola before circling by the new police station back to Mr Agbaje's compound in Ajoyo. Everywhere the ambulance passed, a crowd of mourners followed, their sorrow expressed through traditional dances and mournful songs that echoed through the streets.

The villagers gathered at Mr Agbaje's house that evening for the wake-keeping ceremony. As the night wore on, stories of Mama Enitan's kindness and generosity filled the air, offering solace to those grieving her loss.

The following day, Mama Enitan's remains were taken to St. Theresa Catholic Church for the final burial rites. The sanctuary overflowed with mourners, their grief palpable as they bid farewell to a woman who had touched so many lives.

Twelve Catholic priests stood at the altar in a poignant moment of reverence and as a way to rally around their colleagues. People stood in awe as they watched all the priests carrying out the requiem mass, bending, kneeling and raising their hands as they offered prayers in unison. As the church reverberated with prayers and hymns, the whole village stood united in their collective grief, paying homage to a woman who was once a churchwarden in the same church.

Following the church service, the coffin was solemnly returned to the ambulance and driven back to Mr Agbaje's residence for interment.

The casket was laid beside the grave outside the house, and Akanbi, the officiating Priest, led the burial ceremony. As the burial rites progressed, the officiating Priest declared.

"Now, in this solemn moment, I invite the family and friends to gather around and join in the sacred act of committing Enitan Agbaje's body to the earth. As we prepare to say our final farewells, I ask that each of you, the family members, come forward to pay their last homage, a tangible expression of your enduring love and profound grief."

"I call upon the spouse of the departed soul to step forward," the officiating Priest's voice echoed across the calm ground, carrying with it the weight of shared sorrow and solemnity. As he waited for Mr Agbaje to come forward, he paid his last respect to his mother by pouring the sand on the spade onto the casket.

With a heavy heart, Mr. Agbaje stepped forward, his footsteps faltering yet determined. With trembling hands, he accepted the shovel laden with sand; his grief etched deeply into his weathered face. Father and son locked eyes, their gaze a silent exchange of shared grief and unspoken understanding. As he received the spade from the hands of his third son, the officiating Priest, and paid his last respect to his wife, his emotions overwhelmed him, and his loving children gently supported him.

He stepped softly forward, his shoulders drooping, his two once powerful hands hanging down loosely. On his face were lines of many years of toil now mixed with sorrow.

"My source of strength..." His voice caught in his throat, tears streaming down his cheeks, and his Adam's apple visibly trembling. *"My queen, my wife, my friend. It pains me deeply to bid you farewell. We've shared countless memories and weathered every storm together in our marriage. Through thick and thin, you stood by my side, never wavering, always the last woman standing. You've been my pillar of strength and my rock of confidence throughout the years. A devoted mother to our children and a steadfast partner to me.*

Your wisdom knew no bounds, your resilience was beyond measure, and your quiet strength held our home together. Enitan, if

One by one, each of Mama Enitan's children followed suit, except for Shetan, a poignant tribute to a mother whose love knew no bounds. Despite the physical distance separating him from his kin, his heart remained united with theirs in mourning the loss of their beloved matriarch.

As the ceremony unfolded, Mrs Enitan Agbaje's grandchildren stood together, their faces reflecting both sadness and strength. They joined hands and picked up shovels, ready to pay their final respects.

Working in harmony, they swiftly covered the grave with earth. Each scoop honoured their grandparent's memory, their unity a testament to family bonds. In moments, the task was complete. Standing together, they found solace in their shared tribute, knowing their love would endure like the earth now embracing their grandparent.

Outside Mr. Agbaje's compound, a palpable shift in atmosphere marked the transition from sombre reflection to joyful celebration. As friends, family, and neighbours gathered together, the air filled with the sounds of laughter and lively conversation, a stark contrast to the solemnity of the funeral.

Underneath the shade of swaying trees, makeshift tables groaned under the weight of steaming dishes and colourful platters, each one a culinary delight prepared with love and care. The aroma of traditional delicacies enveloped the gathering in warmth and nostalgia.

Children darted around in playful abandon, their laughter a melodic backdrop to the festivities. Meanwhile, elders exchanged stories and reminisced about times gone by, their faces aglow with the shared memories of a life well-lived.

As the afternoon wore on, music filled the air, the rhythmic beat of drums and melodic strains of traditional instruments enticing guests to their feet. Soon, a spontaneous dance erupted, with young and old alike joining in the jubilant celebration of Mama Enitan's life.

Amidst the merriment, there was a sense of unity and camaraderie, reaffirming the bonds that bound the community together. In that moment of joy and togetherness, amidst the backdrop of grief and loss, they found solace in each other's company, drawing strength from the shared embrace of love and remembrance.

Within two weeks following the burial, Shetan arranged for the VHS tape to be sent to him via DHL, eagerly anticipating the chance to revisit the solemn moments of the funeral rites. As he pressed play and the images flickered to life on the screen, he was struck by Akanbi's composed demeanour throughout the proceedings.

Watching the footage, Shetan couldn't help but feel a profound sense of admiration for Akanbi's poise and strength during such a challenging time. Despite the weight of grief and loss, Akanbi carried himself with dignity and grace, a testament to his character and resilience in the face of adversity.

As the scenes unfolded before him, Shetan found himself deeply moved by the display of love and unity among family and friends, their shared sorrow mingling with moments of laughter and reminiscence. Through the lens of the VHS tape, he was able to relive the bittersweet emotions of the funeral once more as tears flowed down his cheek, finding comfort in the memories and the enduring bonds that transcended time and distance.

In that fleeting moment of reflection, Shetan was reminded of the preciousness of life and the importance of cherishing every moment with loved ones. As he watched Akanbi navigate the complexities of grief with unwavering strength, he couldn't help but feel grateful for the invaluable lessons they had learned from their shared journey of loss and remembrance.

What baffled Shetan till the present was, while he was struggling to recover from his mother's exit, Pa Agbaje passed away peacefully in his sleep five months later, true to his words.

Chapter Twenty Two: The Award

Twelve years after the death of Mama Enitan, Shetan sat down at the podium, his eyes scanning the well-designed hall that radiated an air of academic prestige. The hallowed moment had arrived, and he found himself clad in the highest academic costume on earth. The significance of the ceremonial robe and cap settled over him like a weighty mantle of accomplishment.

The challenges that had punctuated his journey flooded his thoughts. Apart from the fact that the dream was almost truncated when Mr Agbaje couldn't pay Shetan's fees in secondary school, he had a ghastly accident on the M40 with less than twelve minutes to Oxford. He had just returned from Nigeria to London three days this time and was on his way to give his supervisors the outcome of his final primary data collection for his thesis. He almost rammed the Toyota Corolla under the trailer at top speed, save for the grace of being able to swerve in the last seconds. When he read about it online in Oxford Mail the following day, he smiled to himself and thanked the gods of his ancestors for saving him.

The financial burden was enormous as it was a self-financed project. However, the impending recognition now eclipsed the sleepless nights, the debt he has accumulated, the moments of self-doubt, and the sacrifices made along the way. Shetan was on the brink of being decorated with the highest degree in the land—a Doctor of Philosophy in Business.

As he adjusted the academic regalia, and with his wife, Omoyemi, their three children and family members sitting in the hall, Shetan's mind could not help but wander back to the unwavering belief Mama Enitan had instilled in him and his siblings. The memory of her predicting their success, even when their circumstances seemed insurmountable, resonated within him. He felt a surge of emotions, and for a brief moment, tears threatened to escape his eyes.

Mama Enitan, the woman who had been their pillar through every challenge, may not have been physically present, but her spirit seemed to permeate the atmosphere. Shetan could not shake the feeling that she was watching over him, her invisible hand guiding him through this monumental achievement. Similarly, Akanbi, who had pledged to attend the graduation and add to the festivity, could not make it. Having just begun his tenure at a new parish four weeks prior, he required time to acclimate to the community and his surroundings.

The same outfit adorned him was once a shared dream between mother and son, a dream now materialized into a reality that surpassed all expectations.

The anticipation peaked when the moment arrived for Shetan to be called to the podium. The atmosphere crackled with excitement as the master of ceremonies announced,

We are pleased to introduce Feyishetan Agbaje, who has satisfactorily fulfilled all the necessary criteria to receive the Doctor of Philosophy degree in Business. Throughout his education, he has consistently shown outstanding commitment, intellectual achievement, and unwavering determination.

After extensive and meticulous investigation, extensive study, and the creation of an innovative contribution to his area, Feyishetan Agbaje stands before us today as a shining example of the quest for knowledge and the spirit of inquiry.

"I invite you to join me in congratulating Feyishetan Agbaje as he receives his doctoral degree and begins the next phase of his academic and professional career."

The applause erupted, snapping Shetan back to the present, where he stood with his heart swelling with pride. As he walked majestically towards the podium, the audience's acknowledgement of his significant achievement echoed through the hall. The cap and gown adorned him not just as attire but as symbols of victory, resilience, and the indomitable spirit of a family bound by love and shared aspirations.

At the podium, Shetan extended his hand to shake hands with the vice-chancellor. At that moment, with glee in his heart, his memory flooded back like scenes from a movie. In an instant, the memory of receiving an award in his first secondary school streamed across his mind like a vivid projector, merging seamlessly with the present moment.

As they sat in their classroom diligently copying Integrated Science notes from the blackboard, the persistent ringing of the bell startled the students. Confusion swept through the room as they realized an unexpected assembly coincided with the ongoing PTA meeting. Hastily, they joined their peers in a hurried procession to the school hall, where they were asked to stand behind the parents, who occupied only half of the hall.

"Good afternoon, students". The vice-principal said.

Good afternoon, sir". All the students responded in one voice.

"Today, we're doing something different," he continued. "We're going to honour the students who excelled in their examinations—those who stood out in their subjects. This way, your parents can see firsthand those who have truly been exemplary."

"At this moment," the vice-principal continued, "I am going to call out the best student in each class, and such a student should come forward to be honoured and receive his or her award."

Shonu raised his shoulders and smiled, confident that he would be the most outstanding student in his class.

The hall went dead as the parents and students were eager to hear the names.

He started with class four, and the senior prefect, who was also the overall best student, stepped forward to collect his prize. The hall erupted in applause as he walked up to receive his award and share a handshake with the principal—something that had never happened before. His mother was also called out for special recognition, a testament to their shared pride.

Next, the Vice Principal called on the overall best student in year three, known to everyone as Efiko. She was rumoured to study twenty-four hours a day, so it came as no surprise when she claimed the top prize, outshining all her peers in the process.

The entire year two class was already looking toward Shonu when it was time for the Vice Principal to announce the best student for that year. Shonu was beaming with a smile, his expression almost like a new bridegroom's. The Vice Principal cleared his throat, glanced at the name on the list, then hesitated for a moment. He called on the year two teacher to verify what he was seeing, and suddenly, the entire year two class became restless!

"Ladies and gentlemen," the vice-principal continued. "I must commend the overall winner of the Year Two class for his outstanding performance," the VP stressed

At that point in time, Shonu was seen squeezing himself through to get to the front of year two students but paused for a moment to hear the vice-principal call him so that he could walk majestically to the front for the prize.

"If you noticed," the vice-principal continued, "you will see that I have to call the teacher for class two to come and confirm the name on the list. This is because I never expected that, despite this boy missing classes for two weeks due to his inability to pay his school fees, he would still be able to outperform all the others in his" class."

At that point, Evans and a few other students were heard booing Shonu as he was seen looking dejected and sweating profusely. He felt so ashamed of himself!

"Apart from being the very best student, I learned this is the very first time that the same student will win the English and Mathematics prize in year two. I commend this boy for his hard work and resilience," He stated. "Please, can all the students start clapping as I call Feyishetan Agbaje to come forward and receive his award?" He concluded.

That was one of the best moments for Shetan. He could not believe he would shake hands with Mr Faginte, the same principal who hated his poor condition with utmost passion. Mama Enitan was also called forward for recognition, and all the parents gave them a standing ovation. The principal looked at Shetan once again as he returned to join his class; he wondered if Shetan had not been the poorest person he had ever shaken in his lifetime.

However, this memory faded into oblivion the moment he received his award and a firm handshake from the vice-chancellor, which symbolised the recognition of his academic prowess and a profound dedication to the cause that had driven his research—empowering women. The vice-chancellor's congratulatory words were drowned in the thunderous applause that filled the hall, acknowledging Shetan's academic achievement and the impact his research aimed to make in the world.

In that moment of triumph, Shetan could not help but feel Mama Enitan's presence, her invisible hand patting his back, and her voice whispering words of pride. As he exited the stage, the echoes of applause reverberated in his heart, a tribute to his academic achievement and the enduring legacy of a mother's unwavering belief in her children.

The ceremony continued, and Shetan felt a mix of pride, gratitude, and a profound sense of accomplishment. The audience's applause echoed in the hall, symbolising his personal victory and the collective triumph of the Agbaje family. Each step towards the podium resonated with the footsteps of resilience, determination, and the unwavering support of a mother who had believed in her children's potential.

Standing proudly beside his director of studies, who had painstakingly guided him to this remarkable achievement, Shetan posed for celebratory photographs. The admiration in the eyes of his wife, children, and family friends was palpable, their joy amplifying the significance of this moment. It felt almost surreal—a stark contrast to the boy who was on the verge of being written off but now stands as an accomplished academician in a white man's land. The lens captured not just an image but a journey of resilience and triumph etched in the lines of his face, a testament to the transformation that just yesterday seemed improbable.

* 9 7 8 3 3 7 4 1 8 8 0 0 0 *